***Deirdre: The Long Journey Into Legend***

Hours had passed since Niall had last seen the girl run into the forest, but he had no doubt he would find her. And find her he did, it was not difficult; for she was in the very place he had pointed her to. It was near dark when he came upon her. She sat pressed close and half-hidden against a large hawthorn tree near the edge of the meadow. The hood of her cloak was pulled close about her face, her knees drawn up, her brow resting upon them, though her head came up fast enough at his approach. Huddled thus with her cloak drawn closely about her, her eyes large with fear, she appeared to be trying to merge with the tree at her back. The long hours of fear and uncertainty had taken their toll.

Niall stood for many long minutes watching her. Cold, hard eyes examined her closely; from the long, shining red hair that hung in a thick braided rope down her back, her deep gray-green eyes, to the hands that held tightly to the drawn cloak. Small, soft hands that showed neither sign of hard work nor labor of any kind. Her clothes were woolen garments; simple but finely woven and expertly dyed. The soft leather slippers on her feet were simply made and bore no ornamentation, yet somehow they were very different from those made and worn by the women of Niall's clan. These were not the garments of a village woman. Was that why Fedlimid had made off with the others of the party? Were they nobles of the Ulaid, or strangers wealthy enough to pay ransom?

If Niall acknowledged the vulnerability of the frightened woman, no sign of it showed in his face, nor softened his expression, which remained closed and guarded. In fact, Niall's face betrayed no emotion whatsoever. None of the turmoil that stirred within showed itself upon his face. It was not a handsome face, nor was it ugly, but it hid well any emotion that might lie beneath the surface. It was a face of hard, clean lines; there was no softness in the stony set of the jaw, or the grim line of the mouth. His eyes were as hard as polished stones; the color was a brown so pale as to be almost amber, as they gazed down upon the frightened woman. *Perhaps this was the wife or daughter of some wealthy noble or Druid prince*, he speculated. *Perhaps father or husband might part with a sizable ransom for her return.* But it truly was not ransom that Niall thought of as he gazed upon the woman who cowered at his feet.

# Deirdre: The Long Journey Into Legend

by

Katherine McGibbons

A Wings ePress, Inc.

Fantasy Romance Novel

**Wings ePress, Inc.**

Edited by: Elizabeth Struble
Copy Edited by: Leslie Hodges
Senior Editor: Elizabeth Struble
Managing Editor: Leslie Hodges
Executive Editor: Lorraine Stephens
Cover Artist: mpmann



Wings ePress Books
http://www.wings-press.com


ISBN 1-59088-663-1

Published In the United States Of America

February 2005

Wings ePress Inc.
403 Wallace Court
Richmond, KY 40475

## *Dedication*

Believing in yourself is not always an easy thing to do, and the journey through life is difficult enough without adding self-doubt into the mix. Having friends and family who believe in you makes the journey that much easier. This novel is dedicated to several people; my mother, Rosaline, and my step-father, Curtis, who never doubted that I would succeed.

To my friends; Ginger and Kay, who gave me as much encouragement as I needed, to see this through, sometime giving me just that little extra push that was needed to continue on.

Finally, my husband, Jerry, who has been so supportive throughout all these years. He gave me everything I needed to make this novel come to fruition. Without his support and encouragement, I would never have made it to this point, and this novel would never have seen the light of day.

# *Prologue*

*The Legend*

There was much drinking and celebration in the house of Fedlimid, son of Dall. The wife of Fedlimid, though she was great with child, served the men of the Ulaid, and their King, Conochar, for it was a great honor to the house of her husband that the King should choose their home for his celebration.

The wife of Fedlimid felt the child move within her womb, and was stricken with both fear and excitement that her time drew near.

Seeing that Cathub, most exalted of all Druids, attended upon the King, the wife of Fedlimid approached and begged that he place his hand upon her swollen belly that he might tell her of the fate of the child.

When Cathub placed his hand so, the child did call out to him of what was to be. "It is a female child you carry and she cries out to me in sorrow," he said. "A child who will grow to great beauty and charm. A braid of long red hair and eyes of green, small of stature and clean of limb shall she be; however, great sorrow will come to the men of the Ulaid on her account. A great slaughter will take place in her name, and the greatest of Kings will do battle for her hand. You shall call her Derdriu and her great beauty shall bring suffering and shame to the Ulaid."

The warriors of Conochar rose up with a great hue and cry, and demanded the child be put to death, but the King refused.

After the child was born, Conochar would have it that Derdriu should be kept for him until she was of an age to be wed. The midwife let it be known to the wife of Fedlimid that the child had died of the milk fever, and Derdriu was placed into the hands of Cathub, to be raised in isolation, away from all, and educated in all ways as is fitting the wife of a great King.

As the babe grew to womanhood, she did fulfill the Druid's prophesy in her great beauty.

When Derdriu did reach a marriageable age, Conochar sent forth three of his princes, sons of Usna, to bring his bride to him. The eldest of Usna's sons did set his heart upon Derdriu when first he had sight of her. That night he took her hand as his own, and carried Derdriu back to the land of his fathers...

# *One*

*Journal Entry*
*Deirdre McColum*
*The Arrival*

*A confusion of images assaulted my eyes, or rather my senses, being my eyes were rather firmly shut at that moment. Although I did not see these images through my eyes, they were clearly there and as real to me as anything I had ever seen through open eyes. Real, and yet not real, I seemed to pass right through them, or they through me. I could not quite make out exactly what it was I was seeing, touching, feeling. One thing was clear; the feelings, the emotions, which flooded my mind along with those visions; violence, anger, terror, surrounded and assaulted me. Blood red gore, bodies maimed through violence. Phantom figures hacked and slashed at other figures just as unreal. Ephemeral images of marauding hordes wreaked havoc upon each other.*

*And the sounds... sounds assaulted my senses as well. The sounds these scenes brought with them raged around me, touching me, invading me. They pounded through my veins, resounding in my ears, as though the sounds had become... had been made solid, physically real. I felt the screams of anguish. Blood chilling cries of terror ran icy fingers along my spine; demonic, ululant wails twisted my heart and squeezed the breath from my body, and like an insidious voice within my head, urged to more violence.*

*Light and sound whirled around me, pushing, pulling at me. A kaleidoscope of fractured images, breaking apart, swirling within its own specific pattern of chaos, only to come together again to form other, yet more bizarre images.*

*Panic began to rise in my breast, I could not breathe; perhaps I would suffocate. The air was surely being squeezed from my lungs and I would arrive at my final destination a lifeless husk.*

*My sense of time had long ago left me. How long had I been trapped here in this demonic space? Would I be trapped forever here in this place somewhere between what was and what will be, forever a victim to the furious, yet transient images, which inhabited this forbidden space? Surely, the mind, the body, could not withstand this onslaught for long. Would I be lost, fly apart and scatter throughout the universe?*

*Just as I thought I would succumb to the hysteria that blinded my mind and dragged at my sanity, I felt the earth, firm and solid beneath my feet. I wanted to weep; I would weep! I could scarcely believe my eyes. There it was, the ground, fixed and real, though still not as solid as my feet would have sworn. I stomped my foot against the soil beneath it. Yes! Real!*

*An image of one of those ancient explorers flitted through my conscious. Columbus' party discovering the Americas, it might have been, kneeling down to embrace the earth, thankful for deliverance from what must have seemed an eternity at sea. I recognized the need to welcome my return to solid earth. I keenly felt the desire to fall to the ground and give thanks for my own deliverance from what I can only describe as the hell from which I had just emerged. I did not kneel, as those others had, though my knees did wobble and threaten to spill me to the ground. I did not tumble to the earth. Matters more pressing interrupted.*

*The horrendous visions, which had battered my senses through the long and arduous passage through time, did not fade, but rather gathered strength and clarity as my party and I seemed also to be gathering form and mass. Our small group, it seemed, had chosen to appear in close proximity to a pitched and heated battle, quite nearly in its midst. Our entrance upon this scene had not gone unnoticed, to say the least. I had the odd and rather unnerving sensation of viewing another of those painted scenes half remembered from excursions to one museum or another. The picture before me was one of a bloody battle frozen in my mind for all time by the hand of a talented yet perverted artist. Raised axes hung poised and ready to strike through flesh and bone, frozen in the blinding light, which heralded our arrival.*

*Marring the illusion of the tableau vivant, a long broadsword swung, as though in slow motion, through the air; its extreme length and weight carrying through the action, which, once started, was difficult to stop. He who wielded that forgotten weapon stared in awe at the apparition taking shape before him. The boy the broadsword slammed into, for surely he was no more than a boy, stood staring at the specter that was our arrival, his own weapon hanging limp and forgotten at his side, as the blade clove his body. All this passed before my eyes, as if preserved on video and played in slow motion. My own body revolted at the sight, sought to reject what was laid out before me. How could I watch such things and not die myself from the horror of it? All participants in the battle our arrival had interrupted seemed to turn as one to witness the completion of our journey, the final solidifying of our forms and mass.*

*The company of men, motionless on their chosen field of battle, was not a large one, numbering not more than forty or fifty. Their faces, each and every one, seemed to be right there, directly before my eyes. Even now, as I set down these notes, I could easily give descriptions of each man and boy. Their images are burned into my memory for all eternity, their faces frozen in expressions of horror, awe and terror, eyes widened, mouths agape, blue painted faces staring in unbelieving astonishment. Their appearance was equally shocking to me; hair artificially stiffened into unnatural spikes or wild, matted masses, their bare torsos bearing strange symbols painted on chests and arms.*

*I do not know what made my attention focus on one man. Perhaps it was because he did not gape at us in terror or awe. Perhaps it was because he stepped forward, toward me, even as his fellows fell back from us. In his face I saw speculation, intelligence, and caution, even arrogance, but not fear or terror. Perhaps it was his bearing; without question I knew he led these men, at least a portion of them. His appearance was that of any other man on the field, except perhaps he stood slightly taller than those around him, though certainly not unusually so. His face and body were painted as the others. His hair a mass of tangled, braided rusty red, differing from those around him only in color and length.*

*Whatever the reason, it was he that snapped me out of my own paralyzed state, that man who stared back into my own eyes across thirty feet of time and space, quite suddenly raised his sword and motioned me toward him. What possessed me to go to him, I can only guess to have been an instinct to survive I did not know I had. His motion urged me to run and I did, without so much as a backward glance. I raised the heavy skirts of my gown and cloak, and ran. He in turn, began to run toward me, sword raised and I thought, 'My God! He's going to kill me', and yet, I did not believe it and ran on. As he came toward me, he pointed with his sword towards the trees behind him, at the boundary of the field of battle.*

*He passed me, sword passing within inches, raised the small hairs on my arm. I both heard and felt (it seemed) the thud as his sword struck home, burying itself into human flesh. Not mine. Without so much as a pause, I headed in the direction he had indicated. I watched over my shoulder as he pulled his sword from the body of the man he had felled, grunting with the effort, using one booted foot to give himself leverage, arching the blade quickly upward, slicing across the abdomen of another. I watched this as I ran, felt my gorge begin to rise and quickly turned away. I was headed for a forest that seemed to ring the small meadow. I soon reached what I hoped would be some degree of safety, then from behind a large hawthorn tree, tried in vain to see what was the fate of my friends.*

*My eyes raked the scene before me as I searched and searched for some sign of the others, but it was in vain. I could see nothing of my companions.*

*The field had again become a mass of bleeding, screaming, writhing humanity, bent upon its own destruction. Why, in God's name, had we chosen to come to this forsaken place and time?*

# *Two*

*Niall of the Eman Macha*

Dawn would come soon. It was still dark all around, the thickness of the forest hid the red, which even now had begun to streak the sky to the east, but Niall knew dawn was near, it scented the air and left its taste in the mists rising from the forest floor. Head raised, nostrils flared, he drew deeply of the new morning air, letting it fill his lungs and savoring the flavor.

Niall examined the edge of his sword with care in the light from the dying coals of last night's fire. It had been his father Usna's sword, and his father's before him. The feel of the sword never failed to bring Niall closer to his long dead father and his grand sire. In times of battle, Niall took comfort from the nearness of his ancestors. He stroked the traceries etched into the bronze hilt with callused fingers, calling to mind the lined and humor-filled face of his father. Each line, each groove of the intricate whorls and knots etched into the burnished metal were as familiar to him as the faces of his own sons who slept no more than a few feet from where he sat. He would wake them soon and the others as well, but for now, Niall preferred the quiet; time to weigh the conflict to come.

A small meadow had been chosen for the battle. It lay not far to the west of their camp. The men of the Ulaid had been steadily raiding Eman Macha cattle for two seasons. Niall and his men had been unable to catch them on Eman Macha land, until now. One day past, word had come that a Ulaid raiding party had been seen deep within the lands of Niall's people; they were traveling fast and before them they drove eighteen head of cattle belonging to the Eman Macha; the largest number to be stolen thus far. This meadow is where they must cross back into the lands of the Ulaid.

Today men would die; death would surely visit both sides. It was inevitable; Niall accepted this, as did his people. The Druids told them death was not the end, but the beginning. Niall was less sure of this, but he accepted. He had to not only accept it, but believe it; how else could he lead his clansmen, his own sons, to what could be their death? His gaze returned to his sleeping sons. Naoisi, his eldest, just seven and ten years, was already a seasoned warrior and would become chieftain when Niall died or became too old to lead the clan. Ardan, Niall's second son, slept fitfully. Doubtless, he worried about his young wife, just beginning to show the weight of their first child. Just six and ten years, Ardan was separated from Maire for the first time since they had wed just six months past. Niall woke the boy with none too gentle a prod of his foot.

"The men will need waking now, boy. See to it."

"As you say, Da." Rubbing the sleep from his eyes, Ardan emerged from the tangle of his cloak, bright red hair snarled and tangled from a restless night, churned about his head. He kicked his older brother, Naoisi, as he passed on his way to the nearest tree to relieve his full bladder.

Both Niall's sons bore the scars of previous battles on their bodies, as did their father; minor skirmishes fought between feuding tribes. This encounter would be far more serious than any his sons had faced before. Men would die; Niall had to face that, and it was he who must lead them to face death. He was a hard man; the clan must survive, and Niall would do what must be done to ensure they did, even if it meant losing one or both of his sons. Whether or not they survived would be in the hands of the gods, and their own skill with a sword.

Niall dipped the frayed end of a stick into a thick blue paste and began to paint his body with the symbols the Druid had taught him as a boy. The old Druid who had advised Usna, Niall's father, had told his people these symbols would bring them strength, both physical and spiritual, and protect them in battle. Niall no longer believed in these stories, but he painted his body with the spirals, whorls, and animal images anyway. It did not pay to scorn the beliefs of the Druids, even if you did not share those beliefs.

Niall's body held other tattoos, permanent ones. Beautiful, delicate pictures that told a story; one declared

Niall as a member of the clan Eman Macha, another told of his status as chieftain of the clan, still others told of the battles he had fought, and his marriage to Fionna. And then there were those he favored most, one small image for each of the children borne by his wife, including the two that had not survived childbirth; two small stars permanently affixed to the back of Niall's right hand. He had them placed there that he might look often upon his two lost children, especially the last, the wee girl who had taken Fionna into the next world with her. His expression hardened, it did not do to dwell overlong on what was gone.

The men were waking; Niall listened to the quiet sounds they made as they stirred, murmuring quietly to each other. Each man prepared himself as Niall had. They were warriors but also men, men with women and children that depended upon them for survival. Each man reflected on the battle to come and the possibility of his own death and what that death would mean to those they cared for. Vacant eyes stared as thoughts touched gently upon loved ones. Loved ones that waited for their return.

For Niall there was no woman who waited for his return. Fionna had been taken in childbirth these three years past, and though Niall was still young enough to take another wife, his years numbering just six and thirty, he had not. Many had put themselves in his way, hoping to catch his eye. He was much sought after as a husband. Some had warmed his nights, and he had taken them willingly into his bed, though none had taken his heart.

Niall was indifferent to them and though he knew it was time to take another woman, Fionna had been the love of his youth and it was difficult to think of another as he had Fionna.

Fionna had come to him when she was just four and ten, and he but one year older. Young and inexperienced she had been, but she had not been timid. She had taken him firmly in hand and tamed him, taught him what it meant to be a husband and father. Not a difficult task as Niall had given her his heart when first he had set eyes upon her. She and her family had been traveling to the annual gathering of the clans, and had stopped by the village of Niall's people on their way. She had been five years old at the time and six-year-old Niall had first seen her there in his village, and later at the gathering. It was the tradition at such a gathering that weddings were held, babies presented to the clans, and troths pledged. Niall had stepped boldly into the midst of a group of adults congregated together for just such a purpose. Once he had the attention of those gathered, Niall informed his father, and Fergus, Fionna's father, that Fionna would be his wife when she was old enough to be wed. Niall's announcement caused much amusement, but he persisted, year after year, until his twelfth year. Seeing that Niall loved his daughter, and knowing that he was destined to be chieftain of his clan, Fergus relented and the promise was made before the people.

It had gone hard with Niall when Fionna died, his heart had hardened, turned to stone in his chest. He accepted that Fionna was gone, but he would not allow another to cut him so deeply. Never would he allow a woman to turn the cold, hard stone in his chest back into a warm, living, beating heart. He had borne the pain of losing Fionna to childbirth, he could not bear loving, and losing, another. Perhaps he should just choose one; a woman from the tribe who would warm his bed and raise his children. A woman he did not love. Passing his hands over his face and shaking his head vigorously, Niall brought himself back to the matter at hand. There would be a battle today and they must prepare.

Briefly the men squatted on the floor of the forest huddled around Niall as he gave them final instructions. They spoke in hushed tones and had covered the dying fire with dirt; the Ulaid raiding party would now be nearing their location. The Ulaid would not want to remain on Eman Macha lands any longer than need serve and would most likely have traveled through the night. Sounds and smells traveled far on the cold, morning air, it would not do to have the Ulaid aware of their presence just yet. For that reason, the horses had been secreted some way from the camp, with men to keep them safe and quiet until needed for their return to the village.

"Ciran, you will take your party and hide yourselves among the trees."

The mists rose from the forest floor, curling about the trunks of the ancient conifers, insinuating itself through the thickly growing ferns. This was good; the mists would help to hide those of his men that would conceal themselves here in the forest. Hopefully, the mists and thick undergrowth would screen them from the Ulaid as they moved past the hidden men. Niall's own sons were to be among that hidden party. He watched in silence as they found their positions and blended quickly into the surrounding foliage, assuring himself that they would not be detected. He and his remaining men moved quickly to the meadow and across it, careful not to leave evidence of their passing. There they would wait for the Ulaid raiding party to approach.

They did not have to wait long and were soon rewarded as the soft lowing of cattle came to them on the still morning air. Not long after, there could be heard the voices of men, a word spoken lowly, a soft chuckle, a muttered curse. The sounds grew nearer, the raiding party had moved into the meadow. Niall waited patiently, they must be far enough into the clearing to prevent them falling back into the cover of the forest, close enough to give the Eman Macha the advantage of surprise.

Two of his men would take charge of the cattle, driving them to safety in the surrounding forest. At all costs, the cattle must be returned to the clan, these two men would not wait for the outcome of the fight. They were to move the stolen cattle back to the clan's grazing land as quickly as possible. The survival of the Eman Macha depended on it.

The sound of a lark came to Niall; the signal the rear party had closed ranks behind the enemy and was in place. Niall rose and cried out, his battle cry resounding off of the ring of trees surrounding the meadow, a long, ululated cry. The battle had begun. He heard Naoisi's battle cry answering his own, Ardan's immediately after. Niall's heart swelled with pride but also cried out in pain. He wished to go to his sons, to stand beside them as they fought, to protect them at all cost, but he knew they would not thank him were he to do so. They were men now and would see his concern as a lack of confidence in their skills as warriors.

Shaking his head, Niall knew he must bring his mind back to matters at hand or it would be he whose life ended this day. Niall saw that it was Fedlimid, adviser to Conochar, who led the Ulaid raiders. Fedlimid was to be respected as a superior warrior and a man of honor, Conochar on the other hand, was a ruthless and ambitious man. He had destroyed or absorbed many clans in his drive to become the one true king of all the hundred tribes. It would seem that the Eman Macha were to be his next conquest. That would explain the steady raiding of Eman Macha cattle. All the clans indulged in the occasional cattle raid, but the Eman Macha had been subjected to the continual theft of their cattle for two seasons now. Winter approached and with the losses they had suffered, Niall's people would have a difficult time getting through without many dying of starvation; leaving the Eman Macha a prime target for an ambitious man.

Quite suddenly, a strange dizziness overcame Niall, his head swam, and his thoughts became oddly confused and disoriented. He could not focus his sight, causing him to blink repeatedly and wipe at his eyes in an attempt to clear his vision. This soon passed, but Niall felt the hairs of his arms rise, his flesh tingled strangely. Thoughts of Conochar were forgotten as panic threatened to overcome him. *What strange sensation was this?* Niall drew deep breath, consciously trying to contain the panic that tried to take hold of him. The air fairly buzzed around him as though from a thousand bees, vibrated as from an unseen source.

He was not alone in this feeling, all around him men stopped and looked about on every side of them as if to identify who, or what, caused the thrill that ran through them. Just thirty feet from where he stood, the air began to shimmer and blur. Strange noises emanated from the spot, though nothing was there. The very fabric of the air changed, folded in upon itself, and reformed. Blinding white light moved out from the spot, flashing like the lightening that sometimes would streak out of the sky when a storm raged. An image began to appear, the mere outline of figures; five figures.

"Sweet Brigit!" Niall exclaimed. He could see right through them into the still, silently staring faces of the warriors beyond. All moved back, far back, from the disturbance, keeping their distance, but ringing the spot from whence the figures appeared. Niall watched in fascination as these figures clarified and solidified into people; real flesh and bone people. The first man was very tall, ordinary in build, and coloring. A second man, much smaller and with the lined face of the aged. A third man crouched on one knee in front of the two standing. Two women stood slightly apart from the men; one very tall and sturdy, Niall could see hands the size of his own at the terminal end of arms that were well muscled and sinewy, obvious even through the gown she wore. The second woman stood with her face turned slightly away, and was much younger than the others. Five people who had appeared from the air; in dress, very much like any other, although the women, and the elder of the men, wore the simple white cloak and dark indigo gown of the Druids.

They were real, this was no illusion, Niall watched as a freshening breeze lifted the girl's long red hair briefly, then settled it gently back to her shoulders. She turned toward him, the look of fear and unease on her face slowly changed to wonder. She looked directly into his eyes, freezing him where he stood. The women of his clan were big, healthy women, sturdy, ready for hard work and childbearing, much like the tall, homely woman in this strange party. This girl, whose bright green gaze held him, was delicate and fine as the lace ferns of the forest. One hand clutched at the neck of her gown, Niall could see the subtle movement of her breast as it rose and fell with each breath. His own breathing had stopped, held in his chest, and he realized he was waiting to see if they would disappear as quickly as they had appeared. Stranger still, he fervently hoped they would not. Every detail, every feature of this young woman stood out in great detail in Niall's conscious. Without words, she somehow called to him across the distance that separated them, and Niall experienced, for only the second time in his life, the opening of his heart to another.

A movement over her shoulder drew his attention. Fedlimid had taken a step towards the new arrivals. He then took another hesitant step, slowly raising his sword, as though unsure how to proceed, then another step, and another, until he was moving slowly yet steadily towards the new arrivals. Others of Fedlimid's party did the same. Trying to convey urgency without causing panic, Niall motioned for the girl to come to him. She moved toward him at once, without hesitation and Niall urged her forward. Fedlimid's men were nearly upon them.

Starting into a run, Niall watched as the woman's party was overtaken; he did not see what was their fate, there was no time. Others were closing upon the girl. Raising his sword, Niall prepared to defend her; he neither knew nor cared why. She needed his protection and he would give it. His sword swung heavily as she ran past. It struck solidly into the chest of her pursuer, as the man reached out to drag her to the ground. The woman's eyes were large with fright as she looked back over her shoulder. Pulling his sword from the man's body, Niall took down another with the upward arch of the heavy sword, then waded back into the fray, his men close at his back.

The battle raged, building in fury, such a fury that cannot be long maintained, and soon burned out of its own volition. The relatively small group of Ulaid began slowly to fall back, then suddenly broke and ran toward the edge of the clearing in the general direction of their own lands, dragging their fallen companions, those still living, with them. Niall and his men did not pursue them, they had their own fallen to tend, and the cattle had been retaken. Their losses were not great.

Of the eight and twenty clansmen that had followed Niall, six were down. Three of the six lay dead, one of them a young boy engaged in his first battle. A mother would mourn the loss of her child this day and this would lay heavily upon Niall for a very long time. Another would not live through the day. The fifth would likely lose his leg, but would live and the one remaining was injured badly but would most likely survive and without loss of limb. There were others injured, though not so badly; bruises, gashes, and the occasional broken bone. Few men carried swords into battle; most wielded clubs fashioned from tree limbs, or stone celts, which were used to smash limbs or skulls.

Naoisi and Ardan were well and walked at Niall's side among those who lay injured or dead. The Ulaid had suffered similar losses, the dead or near dead had been left behind; six total of the six and ten that Niall had counted at first encounter. There was no sign of the strangers. It puzzled him that Fedlimid would carry off the bodies of strangers, leaving behind his own men; the dead as well as those not yet dead. Dead, the strangers would mean nothing to Fedlimid; therefore, he must have taken them alive.

"Naoisi, I would have you follow Fedlimid. Take three others with you. I would know what he does and if any of the strangers live."

"Aye, Da. Are they from the *sidhe*, do you think? Arguile says they come to take the wee babes from their mams and leave their own changelings in their place."

"Arguile allows superstition to make him a fool, and you can tell him I said so. Now, do as I say, and watch your back, Fedlimid is old and cunning, and he'll expect to be followed. Ciran and I, with a few others, will await you at the camp. The others I will send home to their women."

Watching the boy leave with Ardan and two others still sound enough to travel quickly, Niall thought about what his son had said. Were the strangers sent from the old gods, those who had been worshipped by the Picts, that race of small, brown men who had inhabited this place long before the tribes had arrived? It was said that their gods made their homes beneath the *sidhe*, those odd, rounded hillocks that dotted the countryside. The strangers had appeared to be flesh and blood. Didn't the girl show a good healthy fear for her life? A god would not know fear, nor would one of their followers.

It was a certainty that whoever they were, they were not ordinary folk. Ordinary folk do not walk out of the air. Ordinary folk do not cause the air to crackle and buzz upon their arrival. And ordinary folk would not interest one such as Fedlimid enough that he would run from a battle, taking them with him, leaving his own clansmen behind. It was a puzzle.

"Well its' time to find out who or what it is has arrived among us, isn't it then?" Niall muttered to no one in particular.

Hours had passed since Niall had last seen the girl run into the forest, but he had no doubt he would find her. And find her he did, it was not difficult; for she was in the very place he had pointed her to. It was near dark when he came upon her. She sat pressed close and half-hidden against a large hawthorn tree near the edge of the meadow. The hood of her cloak was pulled close about her face, her knees drawn up, her brow resting upon them, though her head came up fast enough at his approach. Huddled thus with her cloak drawn closely about her, her eyes large with fear, she appeared to be trying to merge with the tree at her back. The long hours of fear and uncertainty had taken their toll.

Niall stood for many long minutes watching her. Cold, hard eyes examined her closely; from the long, shining red hair that hung in a thick braided rope down her back, her deep gray-green eyes, to the hands that held tightly to the drawn cloak. Small, soft hands that showed neither sign of hard work nor labor of any kind. Her clothes were woolen garments; simple but finely woven and expertly dyed. The soft leather slippers on her feet were simply made and bore no ornamentation, yet somehow they were very different from those made and worn by the women of Niall's clan. These were not the garments of a village woman. Was that why Fedlimid had made off with the others of the party? Were they nobles of the Ulaid, or strangers wealthy enough to pay ransom?

If Niall acknowledged the vulnerability of the frightened woman, no sign of it showed in his face, nor softened his expression, which remained closed and guarded. In fact, Niall's face betrayed no emotion whatsoever. None of the turmoil that stirred within showed itself upon his face. It was not a handsome face, nor was it ugly, but it hid well any emotion that might lie beneath the surface. It was a face of hard, clean lines; there was no softness in the stony set of the jaw, or the grim line of the mouth. His eyes were as hard as polished stones; the color was a brown so pale as to be almost amber, as they gazed down upon the frightened woman. *Perhaps this was the wife or daughter of some wealthy noble or Druid prince*, he speculated. *Perhaps father or husband might part with a sizable ransom for her return.* But it truly was not ransom that Niall thought of as he gazed upon the woman who cowered at his feet.

*Why were they here in this wilderness, unguarded, without weapons of any kind? And, what of the strange way they had appeared from out of the air?*

All of this 'what if' and 'perhaps' would get him nowhere. No matter how he reasoned it, she did not belong here in this place. Well, no matter, it was here she was and here she would remain, with none but Niall to decide her fate.

Perhaps it was a reflection of the lowering light, or the tick of a nerve there where the line of a long, curving scar ran close to his left eye; the cold light in his eyes seemed to warm slightly... aye, it did, there was no doubt.

# *Three*

*Journal Entry*
*Deirdre McColum*

*This is it, the moment for which I had spent the last two years of my life preparing. The culmination of untold hours of research into a long vanished, pre-Christian, Celtic society. I spent the last two years doing graduate work at Dublin University studying everything known about this society, their hierarchical system, their language, and their customs. It had not been easy, for little was known about these ancient people.*

*It had also not been an easy task for Walter Daniels, leader of our group, to find four like-minded scientists for this expedition. Finding funding had been more difficult still. The world had moved away from the study of the humanities, art, and culture. Long before my time in the twenty-second century, the world had begun closing its eyes to the arts, music, sociology, anthropology; all obsolete professions in the world from which I had just come. Physics, engineering, computer science, and medical research... genetic research, that was where the money was, that was where research funding was going and those were the professions which had young academics flocking to them.*

*Try to find an academic who would admit to an interest in studying the social interactions of a long dead culture. To do so would mean academic ruin. Well, Professor Daniels had found three of us who were interested in his proposition; Charles Cooper, Ph.D. in Cultural Anthropology, Moira Frasier, MA in Linguistics and myself, Deirdre McColum, BA and current graduate student in Cultural Sociology. The fifth member of our team was Seamus Meaney, Ph.D. in Applied Science, and Professor Daniels' partner in this venture. Professor Daniels also holds a Ph.D. in Physics. Together, he and Dr. Meaney had discovered a way to focus a laser beam out into space in such a way as to fold time. They could target that beam on the specific location where our earth would have been at a specific time in the past, taking with it the molecules of a material object and re-materializing that object at the destination; effectively... time travel.*

*Professor Daniels had tested the machine on himself on three separate occasions. When Professor Daniels and Dr. Meaney contacted me, I was being faced with the hard reality of my own situation. I was a newly graduated undergraduate student in a field that, for all intents and purposes, no longer existed. Funding was no longer available from state, federal or private means. Faculty in my field was becoming non-existent. When these two men told me that I could receive full funding to spend two years doing graduate study into the ancient Celtic tribes of Ireland, and that at the end of those two years, I would be included in a team of scientists that would conduct field research into that society, I leapt at the chance. My adopted parents were no longer living, so there was nothing to hold me back. I sold everything I owned and bought a ticket to Ireland. Actually, Dr. Daniels gave me a generous signing fee, so it really wasn't much of a hardship.*

*I spent the next two years learning the language of the ancient Celts, how they lived, their customs, and their religion. I was even required to learn a little about medicine; we all were. There would be no technology in the field, we would have to know how to survive on our own; at least for the four weeks we planned to be there. Should the need arise, I could splint a simple fracture, concoct basic medicines from local plants and herbs and, God forbid, assist in an emergency appendectomy, amongst other things. Now, here I am, faced finally with that moment which we had all strived toward—and all I could do is stare stupidly into hard, expressionless eyes that glared back into mine, and cower against the tree at my back.*

*He spoke to me in a voice that commanded a response, but the words meant nothing. I gaped at him like an idiot. Two years studying Gaelic, which had not come easily, and nothing he said registered. I had not taken to the language as the others had. It had been difficult for me from the beginning, although the others had picked it up easily enough. Of course, they had all been born and raised in Ireland, with the exception of Moira, who was a Linguist after all, so becoming conversational in a language they had been hearing since birth had presented no problem for them. I, on the other hand, had really struggled, but I thought I had finally mastered the language.*

*I told myself not to panic, it would serve no purpose, but why couldn't I understand him? Had we accidentally materialized in the wrong place? Were we in the wrong place or time? He spoke again, slowly, as though to a dull child. I realized that it was the same language I had studied, just different. The words just didn't seem to connect in my mind. Was it the pronunciation of the words that differed from what I had learned or had the process of sending me careening through time and space done some kind of damage to my mind? I don't know. I am not naturally gifted with languages, it is not my field, and I struggled to understand, thinking I had caught a word or two, but not really. What would I do, how was I to communicate?*

*That and the very real probability that the rest of the team were dead, along with them any chance I might have of returning to my own time, over two thousand years from now, completely undid me. Any pretense at behaving in a professional manner disintegrated as I sat there on the ground, chin on my knees, and my lower lip trembling uncontrollably, tears welled up and spilled over. In the twenty-four years of my life on this planet, I do not ever remember having cried like this in front of another human being; at least not since graduating from diapers. I was totally humiliated, and it made me angry; very, very angry.*

*My heart nearly stopped when he came toward me. I don't know what I expected to happen; rape, murder, I don't know and it doesn't matter. Anger turned to panic. My hand closed around a tree limb lying on the ground, just the size of a club and, without even thinking about the consequences, I swung wildly as he reached out towards me, clipping him across the right temple.*

*I jumped up and made a dash towards the meadow. My intentions were to cross the open field as quickly as possible and hide myself until these men had gone. Then I would find Professor Daniels and the others. What actually happened is that my feet became tangled in the heavy woolen garments and I fell into a muddled heap at his feet. With blood dripping down the side of his face, he reached down, scooped me up off the ground, and flung me across his shoulder like so many leaves in a sack, shaking his head and tsking like a disappointed parent.*

*I can still feel my cheeks redden with embarrassment when I think of myself being hauled into their camp, cursing loudly and pounding at his back ineffectively with both fists. I was deposited on a fallen tree next to the fire with a resounding thump that both jarred my teeth and effectively stopped my verbal attack. A chunk of bread, along with a piece of hard cheese, was thrust into my hands, a small corked jug of some kind of yeasty smelling drink appeared beside me. His not too subtle way of allowing me to compose myself, I assume.*

*He walked to the far side of the fire, crouched down and proceeded to poke at it with a stick. Blood still oozed sluggishly from the wound I had inflicted. I do admit to taking some small satisfaction in that. He continued to ignore me and concentrate on the fire, while I picked at the bread and cheese, stared studiously at my lap, and tried to size him up from beneath my eyelashes. I must acknowledge I was truly daunted by what I saw. Of course, I now recognized him as the same man who had saved my life earlier and suffered a minor, very minor, twinge of guilt at having attacked him. His bare upper torso, still bearing signs of the painted blue symbols I had noticed this morning, was lean, and hard muscled, and decorated beneath the blue paint with finely detailed tattoos. One in particular, on his left bicep, caught my attention; a dragon, or some similar beast, whose limbs were elongated and twisted into intricate knots. I recognized the style as particular to the Celtic art of the era, having seen examples of it etched on gold, silver and bronze artifacts in the Dublin National Museum. La Tene the style was called, after the area where it was this form of art was first discovered. His body was scarred; some of the scars were superficial, others were deep lasting scars, which twisted and puckered the flesh. His hair was nearly as long as my own, rusty reddish-brown, much of it braided and pulled back with a bit of torn cloth. A long reddish-brown mustache framed his mouth. His face was quiet and composed. It was not possible to know what went on behind that mask.*

*Flickering firelight threw a red cast upon the plains and angles of his face and an odd reddish gleam to the amber brown eyes, giving him a demonic appearance, which was most likely largely due to an over active imagination, but even so, did nothing to bolster my self-confidence. Not a man to be underestimated. My gaze traveled back to the tattoos that adorned both arms and chest. I couldn't help but notice how powerful and well muscled his arms were.*

*I noticed that a group of men arrived leading horses. I speculated that the horses had probably been hidden until needed. They would probably be breaking camp and returning to their village soon.*

*"Cad is ainm duit?" His voice made me jump, coming out of the relative quiet of the near dark of the rapidly approaching evening. I am sure that my face must have flamed with the embarrassment of being caught in the act of staring as his body. That, and the sound of his voice unnerved me; quiet, softly burring, totally commanding, although the tone of it was in the form of a question. Still, I could not understand the meaning of his words, though I thought I caught a familiar sound to it. Impatiently, he pointed to himself, spoke one word, then pointed to himself again. Neal. His name! Pointing to myself, I spoke my name to him, Deirdre. His nod of satisfaction*

*convinced me I had understood him correctly and his impatience diminished visibly.*

*Of course, I understood, he had asked me my name. Cad is ainm duit. The pronunciation was just so different I did not recognize the words as I had learned them from Moira. Why had it not occurred to any of us the two thousands years we would travel into the past would have significantly altered the language we had all learned? It had been an unwritten language in this time. Not until the arrival of the Roman monks, still two hundred years from now, would Gaelic become a written language. Time and translation from a spoken language into a written language must have made a great difference in the way this language was spoken. Not to mention that the Gaelic language had nearly died out completely under four hundred years of English oppression.*

*Now that I understood the problem, I would manage. It was just a matter of concentration. It would take time, but I would manage. I would listen to these men as they spoke amongst themselves and I would learn.*

*Tears threatened to return, this time in gratitude for that one sentence I had been able to understand. Wiping at my already reddened eyes, I was determined I would not cry in front of this man again. Then he smiled, it was just a small smile, at least I think it was a smile. More a relaxing of the grim line of his mouth, but I saw the shadow of it touch his face; not just his mouth but his eyes as well. I was unnerved by that expression, coming from a face scarred from war, hard as stone, so suddenly to be touched by a smile, even one so small. Not for the first time, I wondered what lay behind that mask.*

*He left me then, alone by the fire. I couldn't help but notice everyone in the camp avoided me completely, they would not even look in my direction. They had built another fire, several yards from the one where I sat. They fed and tended to their wounded. I wondered if I should offer to help. My medical training was very limited, but I could stitch wounds and make sure they were properly cleaned, or set broken bones. On the other hand, after the entrance I had made this morning, they probably already thought of me as some sort of witch, best not to give further evidence to that notion. So I sat there by the fire for some time, nibbling at the bread and cheese I had been given. My thirst got the better of me and I ventured to sip at the drink given to me. Definitely yeasty, it was most likely some kind of ale or beer. It was cool and wet, at any rate, and I drank it down.*

*The dead and wounded were being placed upon their horses, provisions and weapons loaded; as I had thought, they were preparing to leave this camp. That was when I noticed that Niall and several others did not prepare themselves to depart. As the others left, those who were staying settled down around their fire. The murmurings of conversation was comforting, lulling me into a sense of calm. Or perhaps it was the beer.*

*Next thing I knew I was awake, wrapped up in a large wool cloak, staring up into the sky, what little I could see of it way up there between the tree tops. I realized with a start where I was, and it all came back to me. Our untimely arrival in the midst of a raging battle, the loss of my friends and my subsequent appropriation by the large and imposing Niall.*

*It was early dawn. My head hurt, I never could drink, and I was stiff and sore from sleeping on the ground. I appeared to be alone in a small enclosure of trees.*

*I had been dreaming, a silly embarrassing dream. I had dreamt of being picked up by strong arms and held tightly against a broad, muscular chest, my cheek resting against a leather-clad shoulder. Although the memory of the dream quickly began to fade, I could still smell the rich mixture of leather, peat smoke, and male redolence, and I could still feel the sensual touch of muscular arms holding me. Was it my overactive imagination? Or did I recall the subtle thrumming of a heartbeat beneath my hand, the sensual feel of whiskery growth against my cheek as I reached up to circle my arms around the neck of the man who carried me, running my hands into his thick mass of hair, the beginnings of arousal that quickened the beat of my own heart.*

*Was there more to be remembered? It was all so vague... fading quickly. It was dark, with only the moon for illumination. I seem to remember a face, a dark reddish moustache, hovering over me as I was laid upon the ground. Hands gripped my arms gently, disengaged them from around his neck, then wrapped me tightly in a warm woolen blanket or cloak. A coarse, callused thumb tucked a truant wisp of hair back behind my ear. Then it was morning and surely, it must have been a dream. But, someone had moved me here from where I had fallen asleep next to the fire.*

*I could hear the nearby sound of male voices. The words were muted, but the impatience with which they were spoken was evident. After making some feeble attempt at straightening my hair and clothing, I stepped out from my temporary sleeping quarters, into the company of a small group of men gathered around the now dead fire. It is my guess they had been awake and waiting for me for some time. Of course this is just a guess, although, I venture a very good guess, considering they all jumped up, grabbed their weapons and few provisions, and proceeded to move toward the horses tethered nearby as soon as I had made my appearance.*

*I wanted very much to go with them, it was inconceivable to me that I should stand here and watch them leave me behind, knowing I would be totally alone. The thought of being here in this forest, completely alone, drove me forward a step. When I looked to Niall, his face no longer held the stony mask of yesterday. Now he looked at me expectantly, urging me to decide.*

*But what of my companions, they might still be alive. I had to try to find them didn't I? I knew instinctively the direction Niall and his men were taking was in the opposite direction to the little meadow where I had last seen my companions. It was obvious they expected me to accompany them, why else would they have waited for me to awaken, unless they had some aversion to leaving a sleeping woman alone in the forest. Still I seemed to know deep down that they were all waiting for me to make a move.*

*What of Moira, who had struggled with me over verbs and adverbs? Moira who had spent long hours helping me wrestle with a language for which I was so obviously unsuited. She had mothered me unmercifully; she being without child and I recently bereaved of my own parents, we had fallen into a warm, comfortable relationship. Could I just walk away without knowing what had become of her, and the others? Then there was a selfish motive to finding Moira and the others; if I didn't, I would be stuck here in this time for the rest of my life. I looked back towards where I knew the little meadow lay.*

*Just as I had almost convinced myself to strike off on my own, just as I was gathering my courage and determination to return to the battle site and try to track down my friends, Niall took the decision out of my hands. His hand closed around my arm as he spoke to me in a voice that gave no indication of allowing argument, "Tá fáilte romhat". I only recognized the one word, fáilte, welcome. And really, though the word carries the image of warmth and hospitality, the grip on my arm was firm and relentless, and urged me to follow him.*

*The meaning was obvious. I was not being given a choice; I would accompany them whether I wanted to or not. There was no point in struggling with him, he had made this very clear yesterday. I would have to pick my battles and not waste my energy on hopeless struggle. So I allowed him to lead me deeper into the forest, leaving behind, for the moment, my hope of finding Professor Daniels, and my only means of returning to the twenty-second century... surely, they could not have survived. It was easier to let myself be led, for now.*

*The forest was a beautiful place, once I began to calm down and my fears left me, I allowed myself to look around. The heavy, old growth forest had thinned out into a lovely, deciduous wood of Aspen, Birch, Hawthorne, as well as the old growth conifers, and other varieties I did not recognize. Their leaves had begun to turn with the first color of the approaching fall season. The two boys who rode beside us spoke primarily to each other, occasionally to Niall, but never to me. I was beginning to understand most of what they said, enough to follow the gist of the conversation, although I did not feel comfortable enough with the language to venture into the conversation myself. I doubt my addition would be welcome anyway. Neither of these two boys seemed very happy to have me in their presence.*

*Niall spoke little at first. I rode before him on his horse. Bal the beast was called, as Niall told me, after the Celtic god, Bal of the Evil Eye. The horse had been named thus due to the odd white cast in the animals left eye.*

*Niall's arm encircled my waist, and the other held Bal's reins. His arm would tighten protectively as we moved over particularly uneven terrain. I was uncertain whether the gesture was protective or proprietary. The warmth and strength of his hand as it held me tightly against him seemed to radiate through the thin wool of my gown. I became very aware of the scent I had begun to associate with him; the smoky but pleasant smell of peat, leather and the sensual musky smell of a man. My earlier dream came flooding back to me, bringing with it the heat of blood rushing to my checks.*

*It was a strange, quiet morning. The horse's gait was gently rolling, as I leaned back against Niall's chest, I moved with the motion of the beast rather than against, making it easier for both horse and master to navigate the terrain. Niall began to murmur in a low tone. At first, I thought he spoke to the horse, then realized it was me he spoke to.*

*"The forest is beautiful in the morning light, is it not Cailín?" He held his mouth close to my ear and spoke softly, so his words came to me as a whisper. I cannot think why, but it appeared that he did not want our two companions to overhear.*

*"Yes, Niall. I knew that your country would be beautiful, but I was not prepared for this wonderful lush forest." I tried to keep my voice low, as it did seem important to him that our conversation remain between us.*

*"You have a man, Deirdre? One of those who were with you at the meadow, yes?"*

*"No, Niall, I have no husband."*

*"Your father then, he accompanied you? The woman, she is you mam, yes?"*

*"No, Niall, both of my parents are dead."*

*The words we spoke were banal, meaningless chat, but I could not help but feel there was an underlying, sexual tension that had sprung up between us. The way he held his mouth close to my cheek when he spoke to me. The way his eyes held mine. No longer did he stare at me with that cold, stony expression. He smiled, touched my hand when he would want to draw my attention to some point of interest. Did he feel it as well? Was I reading something into the interplay of conversation, the hand that seemed to move freely along my side, pressing me against him, the way his eyes seemed to seek mine, asking a silent question? Did I imagine all of this? And what on earth was I thinking; anything that might be between us was impossible. Somehow I must locate Professor Daniels and the others and stop this girlish nonsense about a man I had just met.*

*Niall seemed to intuit my thoughts, yet again. "You must reconcile yourself to accompanying me to the village of my clan. It would be dangerous for you to attempt to return to the meadow by yourself, and there is nothing there for you. You will be safe with my people; you will be welcome there."*

*He was telling me my friends were dead. I knew in my heart that this was what he was trying to say without coming out and telling me. There was nothing I could say to this, and fell into silence, though Niall continued to speak occasionally; pointing out a tumble of fallen granite blocks, and an ancient copper beech tree that had to be a couple of hundred years old; its stark, blackened form looking like a devil's trident reaching upwards.*

*The silence of the forest was broken only by his occasional, whispered words. My heart was desolate at the loss of loved ones and Niall seemed to realize this and tried hard to bring comfort. I let him comfort me. This enigmatic man was gentle, comforting and sensual, yet I knew from experience that there was a granite hard, unyielding other within. Just now I wanted to give in to that gentle, sensual man whose arm held me firmly against him, whose breath stirred the fine hairs of my neck as he whispered encouraging words into my ear, whose scent seemed to stir my blood and heat it to the boiling point. I gave myself over to sensation, and turned my brain off, leaning against him.*

*I am not an unfit person, physically speaking. However, I found I was little prepared for this strenuous journey through deeply wooded terrain, and the arduous trek began to wear upon me. I do not know how many hours we had traveled; the morning was still young but we had started while the sky was still dark. There was no path to follow; we were up and down through gullies and ravines, over hillocks, and constantly fighting our way through the undergrowth. At least I was, the sturdy beast we rode seemed very much at home and the hardships of the journey did not seem to faze him in the least. Even my added weight did not seem to hinder Bal as he moved through the difficult terrain. Niall, as though sensing my fatigue, stopped to allow me to rest as we approached late morning. All the others, save the two boys who always seemed near, had long ago left us behind.*

*"You have yet to break your fast. You must eat and gather your strength, Deirdre, we will rest here."*

*The place where we stopped had an ancient feel. A giant shaft of rock had been thrust up through the earth's crust many thousands of years in the past, but that was not where the feeling came from. Scratching in the rich humus that carpeted the forest floor, I discovered that a few inches below the surface there were several logs laid side by side. Looking about me I realized that we had begun to follow what could not really be called a road, but was clearly an established route. An ancient stone-aged road, paved with peeled logs, lay only slightly beneath the surface and had evidently been used for many millennia. Although it was no longer visually present, it continued to be used by the present inhabitants of this country.*

*Even as I sat resting, contemplating the ancient people of this land who, over three thousand years ago, had established a paved route through this primal forest, Niall was there, hovering near. The two boys, I now knew as Niall's sons, Ardan and Naoisi, kept their distance. Then there was a hand on my arm, urging me to rise and continue on, and I think I had begun to welcome his touch.*

*It is nightfall as I write this. Yes, I did manage to make it through the day. We did not catch up with the rest of Niall's men until reaching this camp. I am told that we will reach the village tomorrow. The others now seemed to have accepted my presence. They have yet to approach me and do not seem totally comfortable in my company, but neither do they shun me. They look at me with curiosity and perhaps a little interest, but keep some distance between us.*

*One man, one of those who had not traveled with Niall and I through the forest, seems to be watching me continually. I have caught him staring several times. I believe I heard him called Ciran. He appears to be in his late thirties. I wonder if he has been told to keep an eye on me. Perhaps they do not trust me. It may be they are unused to having women traveling with them, or more likely, they are still curious about the abrupt appearance my group made at their little get-together yesterday. Truthfully, I am surprised they didn't burn me for a witch after our entrance in the meadow.*

*I have spoken to no one since Niall deposited me here upon this flat rock where I sit, close to, yet outside the circle of men that rings the fire. They speak to each other but not to me, although I do catch the occasional curious glance, shy smile, or, yes, out-and-out appraising gaze. It seems as though they are telling stories to entertain each other and I want very much to be part of things. I am feeling very isolated just now.*

*Despite my need for human contact, little niggles of doubt have begun to insinuate themselves into my mind. I am afraid I have more than a few doubts about my decision to allow myself to be led away into the wilderness by these people. Perhaps I should have put up a fight and not allowed myself to be bullied into coming with these men. Not that I fear for my life. They have left me unmolested, and have provided me with food, drink, and their protection, if not their companionship. Rather, I think I let my fear drive me to follow them when I know I should have gone after my comrades, even if it was just to recover the time-travel device. Perhaps I should double back tomorrow and try to find the meadow and the bodies of my friends. I dare not make the attempt tonight. I just don't seem to have the courage.*

# *Four*

## *Into the Wilderness*

"Who are your people, *Cailín*? What do you here on Eman Macha land?"

The woman stared at Niall, uncomprehending. He wasn't sure if she understood what it was he said to her, or was still in shock from finding herself in the midst of pitched battle.

"There's no need to be frightened, no one here will harm you." She did not understand him; Niall could see it in her eyes. A look of sheer panic and confusion seemed to come over her. *Was she dimwitted, defective in her mind?* No, he could see intelligence there in her face as she tried to fight the panic, which threatened to seize control. He would take her back to their camp where she might be less frightened.

"Come then, *Cailín*, let us get you to a fire and food."

Niall should have been prepared for the sudden attack. The signs were there; the frightened eyes, the huddled, hunched posture, all the signs of a cornered animal. And an animal, like a human being, will attack when cornered.

But he had not been prepared. She had taken him off guard, he, Niall, had been caught off guard by this small, insignificant woman. It angered him. The fact she stumbled on her own garments and wound up in a heap at his feet did little to salve his wounded pride. Swinging her up over his shoulder, Niall found himself trying to deal with flying feet and fists, as well as his own anger, which faded quickly away as he fought to control savage little feet. The tirade that poured from her he could not control. Her words meant nothing to him; however, it was obvious they were not words meant to charm or endear. The woman clearly was not singing his praise. He had saved her life and his reward was to have this abuse heaped upon his head.

He set her down rather hurriedly by the fire, built by one of his clansmen, Ciran most likely, dropped a bit of cheese and bread into her hands, then moved well away to give her room to compose herself. He could feel her eyes on him, taking his measure. Niall studied her as well. Though the woman was roughly the size of his own daughter, Levarcham, who was just ten and two, he knew from the feel of her in his arms this was a woman of marriageable age. Slight of frame, thin though not bony, but definitely not a child.

"*Cad is ainm duit*? What is your name, how did you come to be here? Where are your kinsmen, *Cailín*?" There was more he wanted to ask; what was she doing here in this wilderness with only three old men and a woman to protect her. If she was married, where was her husband? Had he been one of those old men Niall had seen materialize in the meadow? She seemed very young to have been given to one so old, but he had seen it happen before. If a man had wealth and substance, even an old man could acquire a young wife.

None of this could he ask, the little he had said had started her trembling, her lower lip shivered and was immediately clamped between straight, white teeth as her eyes began to fill again with tears. Impatience flooding through him, Niall pointed to himself in desperation and spoke his own name. He was instantly rewarded. She understood, and her excitement brought a flush to her pale cheeks and she spoke to him at last. One word... her own name... Deirdre! Then she smiled at him, just the ghost of a smile, which lit her face and brought an involuntary smile to Niall's own scarred face, and another feeling as well, somewhere deep within his loins; the reaction was immediate and physically overpowering.

He had left her by the fire immediately upon learning that one thing about her. Her name was Deirdre. It was enough.

The horses arrived and Niall issued orders. All would return to the village, except a few who would remain with him to await the return of his sons. They would remain here tonight and follow the others early the next morning. The dead and wounded must be returned to the village as quickly as possible.

That had been hours earlier. He had watched as she drowsed by the fire. Fighting to control his body's urgent reaction to Deirdre, Niall found he could not keep his mind from wandering back to her over and over again.

Satisfied that Deirdre now slept deeply, Niall lifted her into his arms, moving her to a small embrasure of trees nearby. There she would be safe from overly curious animals and could still enjoy the warmth of the fire. As he carried her, Deirdre's eyes had opened to look at him, though he knew she slept still and did not really see him. Her arms had come up around his neck and her hands tangled in his hair. Did he imagine she whispered his name? Her eyes opened again as he settled her into the folds of his own cloak, for the night would be a cold one. She seemed to stare directly into his eyes, then was asleep again.

He sat for some time watching her sleep before joining his clansmen at the fire. Something had stirred deep within. It had been a long, long time since he had felt these stirrings. Not lust, Fionna's death had not prevented Niall from enjoying the warmth of a woman's body, but something else.

Ardan, Arguile, and Illan had returned to the encampment; Naoisi still followed Fedlimid and the Ulaid raiding party. He had sent the other three back to the camp to avoid drawing attention to their shadowing of the Ulaid. The conversation around the fire had turned immediately to Deirdre and her strange party.

"This woman is not one of the Eman Macha, Niall. We must use caution. There are strange doings surrounding this woman."

"I do not doubt you, Ciran. I saw their arrival as well as you. More, I saw the look of total incomprehension on this woman's face when I spoke to her. She did not understand my simplest questions. You say she is a stranger to us and I agree. But she is a young woman who has been separated from her people. She is alone and unprotected.

Would you have us abandon her here because of superstition and fear? Leave her alone in this wilderness without protection? And what is it you fear, old friend? A young woman who lets tears fall when spoken to too harshly?" Niall clamped a familiar hand upon the shoulder of the man to whom he spoke.

"I know you are a good man, Ciran. We have been friends since the cradle. You have daughters of your own. Would you have me turn my back on a helpless woman? Would any of you?" Niall spoke this last to all the men who ringed the low, glowing embers.

"Now then, Niall. I did not suggest we should turn our backs on the wee girl. I just said she is a stranger to us and we should use caution, is the thing."

"She is a stranger no longer. I will have her as my own." Niall was as surprised as the others at his sudden announcement. Once he thought on it, he realized it was right, it was what he wanted... she was what he wanted.

"I have long thought I should take another as a wife." Niall's expression had turned pensive. "This woman will do as well as any, her people are most likely dead and she has none to speak for her or see she is protected. When we return to the village, I will take her as my wife with the *handfasting* ceremony; the marriage itself will take place at the next gathering. It is settled." Niall's tone left little room for argument, Niall was not one to be contravened, but signs of agreement were not readily apparent.

It was only Ardan who dared to speak his thoughts, "Aye, well she is of marriageable age, Da, though perhaps it would not be wise to marry with her yourself. My brother Naoisi would be a likely choice. It's time he took a wife and produced you an heir, do you not think, Da? Perhaps Naoisi would be a better choice for the woman?" Ardan's reaction to his father's announcement of his intention to marry Deirdre was mirrored by most of those present. To have their chieftain and clan leader marry this strange woman was not well received.

"Just as you say, Ardan," agreed Arguile, "there are many unmarried men in the clan, and an unwed girl won't stay that way long, hey Niall?"

Others around the fire nodded in agreement. "Aye, a young, marriageable woman will not remain that way long," added Ciran.

A rare find in territories where the clans lived isolated from each other by great distances, meeting only yearly at the gatherings, a woman of marriageable age was indeed a commodity that was not to be ignored.

"I neither asked for, nor wish your advice on the matter, boy. If I had wanted Naoisi to have the woman, I would have given her to him." It was unwise and dangerous to argue with Niall in such a mood. "Mayhap you feel this matter requires I ask the approval of my sons?" Anger colored Niall's words, though they were spoken in a low, even tone, all the more dangerous because of the deceptive calm, which overlay his manner and voice. No one was fooled and none chose to continue the debate.

Ciran it was who hastened to assure his friend none meant to question his right to choose the woman for himself.

His clansmen had often encouraged him to take another woman as his wife. Now they would argue that his choice must meet their approval. His scowl deepened and he grunted out a meaningless rejoinder and, turning his back to them, he settled down to sleep. He had no desire to join in the hesitant, halfhearted conversation his clansmen attempted to carry on as they sat idly around the fire.

The truth was Niall had been sorely shaken by the day's events. Oh, not just the fighting—bad enough—nor the deaths of his clansmen, worse still. Nor was it the unexpected and truly earthshaking arrival of these strangers; all that was bad enough. What came to mind was Deirdre herself and how she had left him more shaken than all the other events of the day. She had not left his mind since he had first seen her appear before his very eyes. Even after the fighting had resumed, and Niall fought for his life, his thoughts had returned again and again to those bright green eyes and heart shaped face. The words he had spoken to his clansmen had not conveyed the depth of desire he found he now had for Deirdre.

This very evening, when he had carried her to her bed and in her sleep she had slipped her arms around his neck, he had wished for nothing more than to carry her further into the forest and take her. He could not do that; taking a frightened woman against her will did not appeal to Niall, although he knew there were those who did not find important such things as a woman's consent. She was not a woman he wished to take only for a night's pleasure. He could not bed her, then walk away from her; Niall would have her for his wife. Therefore, the laws of his people must be observed. They would carry out the *handfasting* ceremony as soon as they returned to Niall's village. This would allow them to live as man and wife for the period of one year and one day. A formal joining ceremony would take place at the next gathering, before the year of *handfasting* ended, making their union indisputable.

It had troubled him deeply when Ardan had suggested Deirdre be married to Naoisi, Niall's own son, although the same thought had occurred to Niall himself... briefly.

No, it was decided, she would belong to him, or she would belong to no one.

Rolling over to his other side, he glared balefully into the dark, adjusting himself into a more comfortable position. He continued to stare into the dark long into the night, in the very specific direction of a small alcove formed by young trees growing in a tight semi-circular formation, where a red-haired, green-eyed woman slept, unaware of the turmoil she had created for Niall.

Naoisi returned during the late hours of the night to find his father awake and staring into the dying embers of the fire.

"Da? Why do you sit here so late?"

"And why else would I sit here awake, but for my son to return safely and tell me what it is he's found?" Why did he suddenly view Naoisi with suspicion, as a rival?

"Are you angry with me, Da? Have I done something?"

Sighing, Niall felt the anger and suspicion leave him, "No, son. It is just weariness that sharpens my tongue. Tell me what it is you have seen and heard."

They sat, shoulder to shoulder, speaking quietly so as not to disturb the others. Naoisi spoke of the Ulaid and what he had learned, and Niall spoke of Deirdre to his son. Because of what Naoisi had learned, Niall was even more determined that Deirdre would remain in his care. Father and son, they were so alike in the soft, red glow of a dying fire. Naoisi watched his father's face carefully, trying to read the thoughts behind the words, but like so often since his mother's death, Naoisi found his father's face to be unreadable. Although there did seem to be something different, the young boy could not identify what it might be. His father seemed more at ease than he had since Naoisi's mother had died. After a time, they slept. Dawn would come soon and they would need what sleep they could find.

The next morning the men sat around the long dead fire, complaining loudly about women who could not leave their beds before the sun had climbed high into the sky. They had been ready to leave for some time and were not happy about the delay, though in truth, dawn was still some time away, and there in the forest, it would be hours before the sun would shine upon them. Niall had sent many on ahead, keeping back only enough to ensure their safety. This was the land of Niall and his people, but there was always peril to be faced in the wild forests.

After two days of uncommonly good weather it was time to be home in their own stone rath before the expected rains came. The village was still two days journey away, two days journey, that is, if the journey was ever begun, and once begun, the pace was a swift one. It was inconceivable the rains would hold off for another two days.

Pulling the hood of her cloak over sleep tousled hair, Deirdre emerged from the trees, to the relief of all those who waited.

A gesture from Niall brought the men as one to their feet. Horses were mounted, and the men waited. Waited for the woman to make her decision; would she come with them? In spite of Niall's announced intention to make this woman his wife, it was still her decision.

Niall could see that Deirdre struggled with the decision; should she follow Niall or try to find her companions? Would it be possible for her to leave here, to follow him and his men, without knowing the fate of her companions?

Niall understood something Deirdre did not, something no one present, save Niall and Naoisi, knew. She could not be allowed to return to the meadow, especially after what Naoisi had reported to him last night. He preferred Deirdre believe the choice to be her own, but it was not necessary. He had already made his decision. He did not wish to share with her what Naoisi had learned, it would serve no purpose, and he was unsure whether or not Deirdre would understand his words should he choose to enlighten her.

Still she hesitated, although Niall thought he saw in her face the desire to come with him. This gave him the courage to give her the little push he felt she needed to make her final decision... and they needed to leave now. Fedlimid would be coming after her soon.

Taking Deirdre's arm firmly, *"Tá fáilte romhat."* The words said welcome, but Niall's tone left little doubt of his intention. She was to come with him.

Deirdre hesitated slightly, then seemed to make up her mind and allowed Niall to lead her to the horses, and into the forest. Niall's mien seemed to demand acquiescence, his physical presence seemed to overshadow any objections, which might be raised, though Deirdre was not only aware of it, but in fact, seemed to find it reassuring. It was much easier to be led, to allow someone else to make the difficult decisions.

Ahead of them, Naoisi and Ardan had stopped, curious why their father did not ride beside them. Only Ardan noticed the bright spark, which had appeared in Naoisi's eyes and the tightening of his jaw as they watched their father approach, Deirdre sitting before him, his arm holding her tightly against him. Throughout their day's journey, Ardan observed that Niall kept well behind his sons as they rode through the forest, his head bent to hers, whispering to the woman. It was obvious to Ardan that the woman Deirdre returned his father's feelings. She leaned into his shoulder as Niall whisper to her. She touched often the arm that encircled her waist, looked up into his eyes as he spoke to her. Ardan had seen this same look in the eyes of his own young wife. Ardan also observed that Naoisi did not miss any of this. It did not bode well.

Niall's heart raced in his chest. Holding Deirdre in his arms, pressed against him, the heat that radiated from her body, the clean scent of roses that emanated from her hair, caused his blood to quicken. Lust clouded his thoughts, it was well that Bal would obediently follow the others, for Niall's thoughts were all to intent upon the woman who rode before him.

He spoke to her of her kin; those who had arrived in the meadow with her. It was best she think they had died in that meadow. Better that Deirdre forget any thoughts she might have of trying to find them.

Early evening, with night not far away, Niall, his sons and their clansmen sat by a slowly burning peat fire. They had eaten and now sat listening to the telling of tales. It was Ciran, well known as a storyteller, who told them of the story of *The Hound of Macc Da Thó*. This story was of a great hound, which stood as tall as the tallest of men and was so fierce it could defend the people of his king from large armies of warriors. This was a great favorite of the men of the Eman Macha, Niall as well; however, this time Ciran did not hold Niall's attention. Niall saw only Deirdre as she sat some small distance from the men, scratching at a piece of leather with a sharpened stick, which appeared to have been blackened at one end. Niall heard only Deirdre, she sighed, the stick she held made soft scratching sounds, and he thought that perhaps he even heard each breath she took. He could not keep his thoughts from her. Niall saw also that Naoisi watched Deirdre as keenly.

"Da, what is it takes your thoughts so far from us? This tale has always been a favorite of yours." Naoisi speaking to him brought Niall's attention back to his clansmen, only to find all eyes upon him.

"Forgive me, Ciran. It is no fault of yours, but this story does not hold me tonight. There are other thoughts that persist in pushing all others from my mind."

"Da, I must speak to you. Now!" Naoisi's voice held an urgency that Niall could not deny. He knew what the boy would ask of him, and he would not have it.

Niall's reaction was swift and startling. His left hand shot out to grab Naoisi by his tunic and pulled him forward until nearly nose-to-nose. "If it's to do with this woman, Naoisi, I tell you to leave it. Don't speak of it and I will not be forced to answer. Deirdre is to be my wife and you will accept it." Naoisi was a seasoned warrior, but still a young man and a son used to obeying his father and chieftain. Niall's sudden anger lent him a terrible aspect that confused and cowed the young warrior. Though he hesitated before leaving, leave he did, his eyes questioning, looking to his father for the guidance he had always received from that quarter, the guidance that was not there for him in this matter.

Standing before Deirdre, Niall addressed himself to her, holding his hand out to her.

"Come, *Cailín*, I will find a safe place for your bed"

Deirdre was unaware she was the focus of the tension she had suddenly seen flare up between father and son, and had not understood much of what had passed between them. She understood only that the father was warning his son off over something and he was very, very angry at the boy.

Taking her hand, Niall pulled Deirdre to her feet; his hand encircled her arm, pulling her with him as he strode to the center of the men gather before the fire. All had fallen silent at the confrontation between father and son. None had ever seen Niall react in such a way towards any man. And they all knew the cause. All eyes were riveted on Deirdre.

Deirdre understood at once her situation had changed dramatically in just these few seconds. Instinct for survival drew her closer to Niall.

Clasping Deirdre's hand in his, Niall faced the men gathered.

"Each of you have made clear to me that you disapprove of my intention to join with this woman. You are kin and clansmen, so I allow you latitude, however, I will tell you now, do not push me. I will have this woman, and I will kill anyone who attempts to prevent it. Has this been made clear?" Now came the deciding moment. He did not show the apprehension that had plagued him. If his men should reject this joining, it could jeopardize his position as the clan leader. If they would not accept her, would he leave the clan for her? The answer, to his surprise, was yes. That would be a last resort. As their prince, their chieftain, it would take much to bring these men to the point of open defiance. Niall was not disappointed. Each man, including Naoisi, showed the shock of his words upon their faces. He could actually chart the emotions that ran through each; first shock, then disbelief, next was consideration, then last came acceptance.

As usual, it was Ciran that expressed the feelings of the others. "Niall, you are my friend, cradle brother, my father attended upon yours as his closest adviser. You are also my prince and my lord. I will follow you as you order and never question your decision, whether be in battle, or in the choice of a woman. I beg your forgiveness for assuming upon our friendship. If you wish to be a husband to this woman, she will be accepted into my heart as your wife, and my lady."

Deirdre had understood a little of what these men had said to each other but had not followed it all, they spoke too quickly and the highly charged emotions of the confrontation made it difficult for her to understand all of what they said. Their words had been addressed to each other and not to her, but she knew with certainty that it was she who was at the heart of this confrontation. There was one thing she did understand, *fear céile*, husband. Why would the one called Ciran speak of a husband? Oh God! Did he ask Niall to give her to him to marry? How could this be possible? How was it she could understand Niall almost perfectly when he spoke directly to her, and not follow these conversations between others? She didn't know, and now was not the time to get into that. She knew only that they all watched her intently. Their gazes were not unfriendly, and certainly not hostile either. When Niall turned and addressed her, she concentrated hard. But he only repeated that he would find her a place to sleep.

Looking up into his face as they removed themselves from the circle of men, Deirdre saw emotion there for the first time since coming into his presence two days ago. It was not exactly fear, nor panic, but perhaps apprehension.

"It is my intention to claim you for my wife, Deirdre. Speak now if there is one who has already done so. Do you understand? Have you a husband, *fear céile*, husband?"

Deirdre understood *fear céile*, and answered with a shake of her head. "No, Niall, no husband."

His relief was clear and Niall repeated. "I would have you as my wife, would you join with me?"

There was only one word she could think of as a response. It made no sense, and even as she said the words, she was astounded with herself. "*Tá*", she nodded her head as she spoke. "Yes, I will have you as my husband." God help her, but yes, she did want him.

His smile was instantaneous and triumphant. Deirdre felt her own apprehension dissolve. Niall's relief mirrored her relief. Whatever else happened to her, whatever else should come her way, Deirdre knew that Niall had committed himself to her and would do whatever it took to protect her.

Still clasping her hand, Niall and Deirdre left the camp, moving away from the group and into the woods. Was Niall intending to start the honeymoon early? Perhaps this was typical for engaged couples. Deirdre forgot her apprehension as she followed Niall into the woods.

Niall watched her face closely; he had already discovered Deirdre's face was much easier to comprehend than her words.

They reached a huge outcropping of rough granite shoving its way up from the ground like a jagged, stony spear. Some tremendous geologic upheaval, a millennia or so in the past, had thrust this rocky monolith upward. The pressure of the force exerted by the earth had formed a crack through its center, two hands taller than a standing man and the width of a man with arms extended. A small stunted tree grew from the mouth of the cave formed by this fissure, shielding and protecting it from the elements. The cave was plenty large enough for two to enter and lie down in relative comfort. It was into this small cave Niall gently pushed Deirdre and entered behind her.

# *Five*

## *Walter Daniels and The Travelers*

The ride was a rough one. More so than any other trip Professor Daniels had made thus far. Perhaps it was the violent battle taking place at the very moment of their arrival, which had caused such an assault to the senses. The last thing he had expected was for a battle to be taking place at this particular time, in this particular place. If he had, Daniels would certainly not have selected this site for their arrival. Of course, it may have had nothing to do with the battle; perhaps is was the large number of people that had been transported. This was the first time he had transported more than one person at a time, and it had definitely been a risk. But Daniels was nothing if not a risk taker.

Professor Walter Daniels was an eminent Physicist, renowned in his field. He had published one hundred and twelve journal articles in his long and productive career. He had four different labs, which included sixteen graduate students, eight research assistants and any number of undergrads. His projects were always perfectly organized. Nothing ever went amiss—it was not possible his calculations could be off. He personally had made this trip a number of times, and never before had anything like this happened. He had always hit his targeted time and place on the nose. Therefore, this must be the correct location. But there was not supposed to be a battle underway in this meadow.

First things first, and most important of all, they must remove themselves from the immediate area. Taking advantage of the few precious seconds of stunned inactivity their arrival had caused, Professor Daniels called to his group. "Right people! Lets be off," he shouted, "this is not the best place for us just now, is it then?"

As a group they started off towards the edge of the forest, but were soon surrounded by large men with weapons. The chaos of the moment, shouting, shoving, the sight and smell of blood soon overwhelmed them.

Before they could collect their thoughts for an organized escape, a body of men surrounded each of the travelers. No one actually attacked them, they were never threatened with bodily harm; it was more like they were being herded, shoved along towards the fringe of the battle, away from the actual fighting. The tide of the battle turned and they were swept along with the retreating forces. The momentum carried them from the field into the forest, and quite far into the wilderness. They must have been hustled several miles into the forest and it was closing onto dark before a halt was called. His group scattered, Daniels looked about him in desperation. Where on earth could they be? Battle bloodied men milled about on all sides, but all kept their distance from the slight, graying man dressed in Druid robes.

~ * ~

Moira Frasier hurried up to him as he searched; two men with drawn weapons followed, herding her towards Daniels. Moira limped noticeably. "I believe I've twisted me bloody ankle, Walter. Some sodding little twit thought he was going to get lucky. Well, you can believe his sodding family jewels are up around his bloody Adams Apple right now. Dropped me like a sodding hot potato, he did!" Moira had grown up in the East End of London and in moments like this, her Oxford cultivated speech would revert back to the vernacular of her youth... not that any of them had ever encountered, or had ever expected to encounter, moments like this.

Seamus Meaney and Charles Cooper were next to rejoin the group. They also were accompanied by their own personal security guard. Deirdre's absence was immediately noticed and they all then spread out to look for her. She was nowhere to be found. *Where was Deirdre?* They realized they had not seen her since the moment of their materialization. Could she have been killed on the battlefield? No! No, he would not even entertain the thought of it. It was inconceivable. Perhaps she had been carried off by one of the barbarians. Dear God! Perhaps she was being molested at this very moment! *Don't panic*, Professor Daniels commanded himself.

Anger soon replaced panic. Casting about him, Daniels spotted the person he was looking for, the others following at his heels.

"Fedlimid! You fool, where is she? What were you thinking, engaging in a battle in the very place Conochar ordered you to meet us?" He knew his calculations had been correct. Witness the fact that Fedlimid had been there in the very spot Daniels had requested he meet them. "Do you realize the consequences of your actions here today?" Grabbing Fedlimid by the gold torq that encircled his neck, Daniels, who barely came up to the big Celts shoulder, shouted into the man's face, spittle flew from his mouth and his hands shook with rage. "One of your men must have her. Find her now before she is harmed."

"Aye, Lord Cathub, are you certain she is not here?" The look on Daniels' face was enough to catapult him into action. Signaling to several of his men, Fedlimid sent them off to search for Deirdre.

"Lord Cathub?" Moira interjected, "Walter, why has the man called you Cathub?"

"Walter?" It was Seamus Meaney, Daniels' partner in the time-travel project, who spoke at the same time as Moira. "Do you know these men? Who is this Conochar you spoke of, and what has all of this to do with our project?"

"Well now, you don't think I would have brought you all here to this place without planning for your safety, do you? You all know that I have tested the time-travel device on myself several times. So, on my first trip back in time, I happened to make the acquaintance of his lordship, Conochar, High King of Ireland. I established myself in the identity of Cathub, Druid priest. I thought it best to have allies in high places, just in case we should run into trouble, as we have, have we not? What better guise than that of a Druid priest, they are feared and respected. Their word is accepted as gospel, so to speak. I had arranged with Conochar to send Fedlimid and a small group of warriors to this place so that we would not have to travel unprotected."

"So what did happen? Why did we land in the middle of some bloody battle?"

Before he could answer, Fedlimid returned from organizing the search for Deirdre. Hearing Moira's question, he sought to explain.

"Lord Cathub, it is unfortunate the Eman Macha chose this time and place to attack. It was completely unexpected. We did our best to protect your lordship and your followers. We did all we could to get you from the field and remove you from all danger. I had ordered a group of men to surround and protect each of you until you could be removed from danger. You can not know..."

"I know exactly what happened, you fool. You arrived at our meeting place early by a few days and decided to conduct a little cattle raid to pass the time, is it not so? It is your actions that have brought this catastrophe down onto us all, yes? If the girl can not be found, I will see to it that Conochar deals with you severely."

"It was Conochar who ordered the raid on Eman Macha cattle. We were sent three days early for just that purpose. You know Conochar has long desired to bring the Eman Macha under his control."

"That fool! His ambition and greed may have cost our girl her life. Where are your men? Why do they not report back?"

"I will check, my lord."

"Walter, what has happened to Deirdre?" Moira asked. The girl was as dear to her as any daughter she might have had. "She was right beside me when we—"

Fedlimid encouraged one of his men forward with the point of his broadsword then shoved him forward to stand before Professor Daniels. "My lord Cathub, this man was one of four who was to have secured the Lady Deirdre and carry her to safety. He has a story to tell, my lord."

"Niall of the Eman Macha has taken the young lady, my lord. Lomnae and Braion both were cut down with his sword as they attempted to secure the lady's safety."

"And what of you?" Daniels eyed the man suspiciously. "Where were you when your fellows were dying for their duty?" The man's expression was sullen and he refused to look the Druid in the eye.

"It is not my fault, my lord. She ran the wrong way." His hand appeared to start toward his own sword, but he apparently thought better of it, odds not being good that he would be able to extricate himself from the situation with his sword. Everyone knew of and feared the Druid priest, Cathub, especially after the incident they had just witnessed this day.

Daniels addressed himself to Fedlimid, "You will take us back to the meadow. Deirdre must be found and her safety ensured. Who is this Niall of the Eman Macha? Would he harm her?"

"Niall is a man of honor, my lord. He is a minor prince of the Eman Macha, chieftain of his clan, and would consider it his responsibility to see to her safe disposition. The lady will come to no harm at his hands"

"Disposition! Walter, what does he mean disposition?" Moira definitely did not like the sound of that.

"Yes, What do you mean by disposition?"

"She is a young, marriageable woman, with no male kin to see to her protection. He would most likely try to find a husband for her as quickly as possible. A young unmarried woman can cause trouble, especially among the unmarried men. He would want to avoid that at all costs."

"Dear God! Walter, we must go and find her now. We cannot allow her to be married off to some bogsman. We are responsible for her being here. We must stop this at once." This came from Charles Cooper, his exclamation brought an affirmative response from the others.

"Charles is right, Walter. We cannot allow Deirdre to be married off like this. Oh Lord, things could not have gone more badly." Moira interjected.

"Of course, of course." Trying to calm his fellow travelers, Daniels turned to Fedlimid, "As I said, you will take us back to the meadow at once, there we will determine whether or not Deirdre has been carried off by this Niall person." To Moira, Meaney and Cooper, he said in English, "You must call me Cathub here. That is the identity I have established and these people will become suspicious if you call me by any other name."

"My lord Cathub, it is full dark now. Would it not be best to rest the men, start out at first light, then if Niall and his men have Lady Deirdre, we can plan our attack to our advantage. We saw no sign of horses, they can not get too far ahead of us." Almost to himself, Fedlimid added, "But we will require more men. I will send to Conochar for more warriors."

"Very well, if you think this the best course of action." Indecision nagged at him, and wringing his hands, Cathub continued, "If you really believe Deirdre will be safe and unmolested with this Niall of the Eman Macha, we will do as you say. But we will not send to Conochar just yet. We may well be able to handle this without alerting Conochar of *your* incompetence."

"No Walter... I mean lord Cathub, if we delay until morning, these Eman Macha will have a full day's journey to their advantage." Seamus Meaney spoke up this time.

"They will take their rest through the night and the wounded will need tending. Also, they will be driving several head of cattle before them, which will slow their progress. Without horses, we will catch them easily." The reply came from Fedlimid. Fedlimid was a well-respected warrior and adviser to Conochar. Cathub must rely upon his good judgment to get them out of this mess.

"We will follow Fedlimid's advice. When morning comes, we will rescue our girl. Try not to worry so, Moira."

# *Six*

*Journal Entry*
*Deirdre*

*The rains came during the night. The sound of it pounding against stone, muted as it was, woke me from a restless sleep. If sleep you could call it. I had not been forced to defend my honor, nor had I even been given the choice of enduring... or welcoming Niall's advances. Moira had always said my face gave me away. Niall had taken one look at my face through the gathering darkness, turned on his heel, and left the cave. He started a small fire and settled down before it.*

*I had pouted for sometime at being left so abruptly, without even a token attempt at seduction. After all, I had just agreed to marry the man, and had finally lain down to a fretful sleep; sleep, which had been cut short by the rain.*

*Peering out into the dark, I just made out his shape through the darkness and pounding rain as he sat hunched over the dying fire. I couldn't just leave him to sit there in that drenching rain... could I? So, I called to him to join me in the shelter of the cave.*

*It's funny, isn't it? How relative are things. Outside, in the comparative openness of forest and woods, Niall seemed to be the size of any man. As he entered the cave the size of the man increased disproportionately, filled my imagination, as his shadow, merely a darker patch against the darkness of the night, filled the entrance to the cave.*

*He whispered my name and I would admit here on these pages, my heart raced at the sound. I responded to the caress of his voice with his own name and no sooner had it left my lips than I felt his hands on my shoulders, pressing me back to lie beneath him, his mouth against mine. Somehow, in the seconds... split seconds had passed from his entrance at the mouth of the cave to his body pressing against mine, he had shed his drenched clothing. I can still feel the heat of his bare skin against the tender flesh of my palms, breasts, and thighs. Wet, cold curls tangled in my fingers, dripped rain upon my bare skin.*

*His mouth had sought mine with a hunger that was matched by my own. Strong hands reached beneath me and raised me up to him, my legs wrapped about his waist, as his mouth found its way from my mouth, down to the hollow of my throat, then sought the valley between my breasts. My back arched as the hot, moist, searching mouth found each breast in turn, toying with the nipple that bulleted at his touch.*

*Wet tendrils of rusty red hair lay against my breasts as hot breath and hot, wet tongue blazed across the delicate flesh of belly and inner thigh. The muscles of my abdomen even now clench and spasm remembering the scorching, seeking hunger, the need that thrust itself at me, wanting fulfillment.*

*I can tell myself now, in the dark, waiting for the light of another cold dawn, what happened was due to the fear and apprehension of the previous two days, and that I was responding to the primitive instincts of the female of the species to offer herself to the alpha male, in return for protection. But if I am to be truthful to myself, I must admit what happened was because I wanted him, as simple as that. His cries of release... of lust, still echo in my ears and those phantom cries turn my knees weak and cause my blood to burn.*

*It is not yet dawn; at least the light has not yet reached the interior of the cave, although I can see well enough. I watch him sleep. In this state, his face loses that harsh, grim stoniness. He stretches and growls, not in anger but contentment. Contentment that I gave him. If that statement sounds smug, then so be it. I do take some satisfaction in the pleasure I was able to give to this man in return for the pleasure his touch gave me. Though his body is scarred, it is a pleasure to look upon. It is for all these reasons; the desire he seems to have stirred in me, the pleasure, the warmth and feeling of protection, for all of these reasons, I must not stay with him one moment more.*

*And so, I will leave now, before he stirs, and try to retrace our journey of yesterday. I will attempt to return to the meadow where all this began and find the bodies of my friends; Moira, Professor Daniels and the others. Perhaps I will also find the device that will return me to my own time. I cannot stay here. I do not belong in this place, yet I fear it would be all too easy to lose myself to it and this man!*

# *Seven*

## *Flight*

It was the look on Deirdre's face, which had driven Niall from the cave. It was not terror, not fear of him he saw there, but the seed of desire. He was willing to wait for the seed to take root and grow. Hopefully, it would not take too long; Niall's own need was growing... painfully. He settled himself by the fire, confident Deirdre would call to him to join her. As the hours passed, Niall's confidence waned. Perhaps he had been mistaken and it was not a desire to join with him he had seen on her face. But no, Deirdre had agreed to the marriage, she would come to him.

Sleep, however, was not for him this night, and so he contented himself with erotic fantasies of what would soon be his to discover. The pleasures to be found beneath a shapeless, woolen gown. His mind conjured up an image of ripe breast and flat, silken skinned belly, shapely legs with downy crisp curls of flaming red between them, which parted... Perhaps this was not the best course of action as it served only to bring his need more urgently to hand. Not even the sudden down pouring of cold, driving rain seemed to dampen the fever, which had taken hold. *This*, he thought morosely, *will be a long night...*

Lusty thoughts of naked bodies and mindless coupling were interrupted by the sound of Deirdre calling out to him. Sightless, Niall groped his way through the darkness of both the night and his own thoughts, into the dark, still interior of the cave in blind response to her voice.

Tunic, braecs and boots were shed in haste. Somewhere in the dark recesses of his mind, back behind the red haze of longing that effectively deadened most of his thought processes; Niall realized... knew, he should go slowly. She might be untouched; he might damage her, or worse, instill a fear of carnal union forever.

But the thought was lost to him as his mouth closed upon hers and felt the urgent response he found there. Her hands touched him, took possession of his body, driving him beyond thought, urging him into a frenzy of possessing the soft, responsive flesh which lay beneath him, urging him on until there was no thought at all, only the blood which pounded, pounded, pounded in his ears and through his veins.

Some thoughts slipped through, sliding across his consciousness to be quickly lost. Not a virgin... this did not surprise him. Celtic women would often try on one lover after another until finding the one to which she wished to be bound.

He learned that should he touch her there, it would bring lusty groans of pleasure. He would do so again. Yes... pleasure.

Should he touch the tip of his tongue just there, the muscles of her belly would flutter and quiver, she would tug at his hair with tangled fingers.

Her scent was not the same as other women he had possessed. Niall pressed his face against the softness of Deirdre's belly and inhaled deeply. The scent of her filled him, seeped into his flesh and elicited a responsive clenching of his testicles and an involuntary, and satisfying, completely mindless, thrusting. He was completely consumed by her, the way she smelled, the way she felt and tasted. All of these things were burned into his senses. Hands, mouth, tongue, all of his body, all became instruments intended only to give this woman pleasure, to bring forth cries of excitement, surprise... lust, which in turn fueled his own mindless search for the sensual pleasures of her body.

The full light of day flooded the stone cave bringing Niall up from the depths of shadowy dreams of naked flesh and the smell of Deirdre. Even before he opened his eyes, he knew she was gone. The scent of her still lingered on his skin, but it was gone from the surroundings. She had been gone for some time. The realization that her scent had become familiar to him long before last night's pleasures was overshadowed by the realization she had left him several hours previous.

The men of Niall's party would also have left long ago. They were mere hours from their village and Niall's clansmen, believing him to be indulging in the pleasures of his soon-to-be wife's body, would have broken camp at dawn and hurried on to the village without disturbing them, hoping to reach the village before the rains of last night returned. There was no hope for it, he must go after her alone, a full day would be wasted if he were to continue on to the village for help and Deirdre must not be allowed to find the thing for which she searched.

## *Eight*

### *Betrayal*

Night had fallen. The company of warriors shared out their provisions, and all had eaten, then rolled themselves into their robes and fallen asleep. All but the small group of time-travelers. Each was deep in their own thoughts; thoughts of Deirdre. So involved were they in unsettling images of the many possible fates that may have befallen their youngest and most vulnerable member, none noticed when Cathub, for they all had begun to think of their leader by that name, left their small circle and slipped into the surrounding dark.

If they had noticed him leaving their presence, they might have wondered at the need for such stealth. They might also have wondered at the direction he took; not toward the site of their earlier arrival. That might have made sense; he might have decided not to wait until morning to setout to find their missing charge. No, in fact the direction he took was directly opposite. One might have wondered indeed, had anyone at all taken notice.

For instance, someone who might have followed their flight from the meadow. Someone who might have been observing quietly from a hidden spot just out of range of the light cast by the rapidly dying fire, someone who had been instructed by his father to watch, observe and report back. Someone, perhaps, like Naoisi.

As Cathub quietly slipped into the forest, a silent shadow dogged his steps. When Cathub met with another who had slipped just as quietly from the sleeping company of men, his silent shadow was there to observe.

“Fedlimid, it is imperative that Deirdre be found before any marriage, or any other unacceptable fate, should befall her. I am telling you this to save your life, as well as mine. This is the woman who is to be the bride of your lord and mine; Conochar, High King of Eire. It is she who is to be your queen.”

“My lord Cathub, I had no idea. Conochar did not tell me who the lady was, only that her safety was to be secured. We will find her. I promise you.” Fedlimid began to perspire freely, in spite of the cold night air. The hand that gripped the mantle draped about his shoulders shook every so slightly.

“You had better. Do you have any idea what your fate will be, and mine, should anything befall her?”

“My fate! I care nothing for my fate, my lord. If this is truly the betrothed of my king, I would willing lay down my life to find her.”

“Very admirable.” Sarcasm dripped from Cathub’s voice. “But this does little to help in finding Deirdre.”

“But, my lord, why did the lady run from us? Why would she choose to run to the Eman Macha? We carry lord Conochar's colors, surely she would have known to come to us?"

"She does not know that it is her fate to be married to lord Conochar. And there is no reason for her to know until she is safely within Ulaid lands and under the control of Conochar. Then, and only then, is she to know of the marriage. If she were to find out too soon, she would, undoubtedly, do everything in her power to prevent it. Deirdre trusts me to guide and protect her and it must remain that way until it is too late for her to do anything to prevent this marriage."

"It is a mystery to me. Why would she not want to be married to the most powerful man in all the hundred tribes of Eire?"

"Because she is headstrong and independent. She would find marriage to Conochar abhorrent. But her wishes do not come into this. Through her marriage to Conochar, I will ensure my position and power. Conochar has promised me great wealth to deliver his bride to him and I will not allow the whims of one girl to thwart me. I repeat, she must not know of her fate until it is too late for her to do anything about it. Find her, do not harm her, but bind her if you must, and bring her back under my control. You do this for me and I will see that you become a very wealthy man."

# *Nine*

*Journal Entry*
*Deirdre*

*Cold, wet and hungry, I spent the better part of yesterday trying not to get lost; my sense of direction is pretty bad so I had to backtrack several times before finally finding my way here to this tumbled down fall of granite stones. I remembered having passed it on our way through, just before leaving the deep forest, the day before yesterday.*

*Remembering our journey through here brings with it other memories. That of large, calloused hands with the ability to bring so much pleasure, and wet, rust-colored hair trailing across my breasts. Hot breath against my neck and breasts, heavily muscled thighs... Oh God, what am I doing? I know I must continue on to find Professor Daniels and the others, but I cannot seem to keep my mind from going back to Niall and the way it felt to have him touch me. I want so much to turn around and go back the way I have just come, find Niall and curl up in his arms.*

*I must get my mind back to the matter at hand.*

*The on-again off-again rain has hampered my progress. It was nearly dark when I finally found my way here and decided to spend the night under what little shelter it afforded. But I'm more than halfway there now and one more day of trekking through this forest should find me back at the meadow before noon. I hope. It was only by the grace of God I managed yesterday to avoid running right into a group of hunters, or perhaps it was a raiding party out to steal cattle. I had just located a small ravine I remembered us following part of the way, the day before.*

*Due to the heavy rain, I was walking in the ravine, rather than beside it, because the trees, which grew close by the banks, afforded some shelter from the downpour. I thought I heard the sound of voices and crept up close to the banks of the ravine. Under cover of some thick undergrowth I saw several men headed in the direction from which I had just come. I was concerned about being spotted, so I pulled the hood of my cloak closer over my face and, head down, hunkered down into the dense vegetation and waited for them to pass. I waited a good fifteen minutes after hearing the last of them pass before continuing. Once I had found my way here to this giant building block tumble of rocks, I knew I could orient myself well enough to find my way back to the meadow. But it had grown too dark and I decided to spend the night here and start out fresh in the morning.*

Well, it is now morning, and I'm wet and chilled to the bone. I haven't eaten since the night before last and have had only what water I was able to find collected on leaves and such, and while I had gone to sleep last night determined to press on and find the others, a disturbing thought has only just occurred to me. What if the people I had hidden from in the forest yesterday were, in fact, those I was trying so hard to find? What if they had not died in the battle? What if they had enlisted others, people from a local tribe, to help them search for me? I may very well have hidden from my own friends in a misguided belief that they were dead, or beyond my ability of find them.

Should I go back? If I do, and it turns out not to have been them, I have wasted valuable time, and I may meet up with total strangers, strangers who may not be so kind as Niall and his people. Speaking of Niall, if I do turn around and go back, he may find me before I can determine if it was Professor Daniels, Moira and the others I passed in the forest. Then what would I do? I wouldn't be able to explain it to him. He would probably just throw me over his shoulder again. Not that that isn't sort of an exciting prospect, but I can't think about that right now. I shouldn't think about that. I shouldn't be thinking about Niall at all, except that he keeps creeping back into my thoughts. His touch, his smell, that rich male scent which I swear I can conjure up so easily. Just as I can still feel his hands on my...

I have to stop thinking about him. I have to decide what to do about continuing my search; back the way I just came, or forward? It is a conundrum, and not only that; thinking about it makes me feel a bit sick to my stomach. What if, what if, what if? I have decided... forward! Or rather, back... back to the meadow.

I'm not quite sure what I will do if I get there and don't find anything. No friends, alive or dead, and no sign of where they might have gone. Then I won't know if it was them I passed, or if Niall's enemies carried them off. I will just have to face that when I get there. Besides, I feel certain Niall is probably following me, and undoubtedly will catch up with me. I only hope to avoid being found by him until I have had a chance to reach the meadow and determine once and for all if there is any chance of being reunited with Professor Daniels, Moira and the others.

# *Ten*

## *The Hunting Party*

Niall drove his horse quickly through the forest. She had several hours lead on him and the distance between them increased by the minute. The rains both helped and hindered Niall in his attempt at tracking Deirdre. In places the soft, rain-soaked ground provided obvious evidence of her passing, while other times the rain eradicated all trace of her and he was forced to spend valuable time crisscrossing the area where he had lost her track until he would finally find a place where the forest floor would again reveal her passing, and he would be able to take up the hunt again. He knew, of course, where she was headed, but Niall was desperate to catch up with her before she reached the meadow, or before the Druid Cathub and Conochar's warriors happened upon her.

It would not matter to Conochar that Deirdre was now promised to Niall to be his wife. Conochar would take what he wanted and, from what Naoisi had told him, Conochar already considered Deirdre his possession. Niall must find her and tell her what Naoisi had learned. It had been a mistake to keep this information from her. Although his intentions had been in Deirdre's best interest; to prevent her from learning of the betrayal of someone she obviously considered a friend and protector, he knew now that this seemingly timid and frail woman was actually headstrong and independent and quite capable of determining her own destiny. Naoisi had told him the Druid Cathub used the same words to describe Deirdre, but Niall did not think of her as someone that must be controlled, only that she was running towards betrayal, and he was at fault for not warning her.

He also encountered the group heading in the direction from which he had just come. Also as had Deirdre, Niall and his horse melted into the dense forest flora upon hearing their approach, waiting until they passed. Unlike Deirdre, Niall knew with certainty that those she believed to be her friends were among those that penetrated ever deeper into the lands of the Eman Macha. He watched them pass; the old Druid, now known to him as Cathub, adviser to Conochar. This one walked with Fedlimid, at the head of the party. The woman he heard referred to as Moira, and two other men, who may have been kin to Deirdre... this was not certain, although he did hear them speak her name in kindness and concern for her safety as they passed Niall's hiding place. They walked surrounded by Fedlimid's men, almost as though they were captives being led to imprisonment. Although it could have been for their protection, he did not think it so. It appeared more that these armed men were keeping the strangers contained, rather than seeing to their safety.

This was something to be puzzled over. Was it possible that not all of Deirdre's people were plotting against her? Naoisi had not mentioned their involvement in Cathub's deceit, only their concern for her safety. Yes, it made sense. These others were not part of the treachery of Cathub, and therefore, not being part of the plot, he would have them watched carefully so they could not reveal his plan to Deirdre, once he found her.

He was able to move more quickly once the hunting party had passed him, for Niall was convinced that a hunting party they were, except that it was Deirdre they hunted.

He would go directly to the meadow, and if he did not find her there, he would backtrack until he did find her. Niall was determined to do his best to explain to Deirdre what Naoisi had learned of the treachery of the Druid, Cathub. The fastest way to the meadow, was the way they had come, past the granite fall.

# *Eleven*

## *The Truth At Last*

"My lord," it was Fedlimid who interrupted Cathub's dark thoughts. "There are definite signs that a woman spent the night here. Lady Deirdre do you think?"

"A brilliant deduction, Fedlimid." *Sarcasm was beyond the man's limited intelligence,* Cathub thought.

The search for Deirdre had not begun well. By the time they had arrived at the Eman Macha campsite, Niall and his men had struck camp and from what Fedlimid's trackers told him, had several hours head start. They wouldn't have had such a huge lead on them but for the incompetence of the trackers to begin with. They had failed to find Niall and his men at the meadow, where Fedlimid was sure they would camp. Further, it had taken entirely too long for the trackers to find signs of their passage, and to finally discover where they had camped.

"There is no sign of violence; the lady Deirdre must have accompanied these men of her own accord." This news did nothing to improve Cathub's mood.

"Walter, this is good news, our Deirdre is unharmed. If we hurry on, perhaps we will catch up to them before something does happen to her." Moira had drawn close to the two men as they spoke.

His brow drew together in consternation at the interruption, the Druid know as Cathub turned on Moira with a snarl as he spoke to her in English to ensure the privacy of their conversation. "I told you to call me Cathub. Are you too stupid to understand so simple an order? And what do you mean by sneaking up on me and eavesdropping on my conversation?"

Switching back to Gaelic and turning to Fedlimid, he barked an order, "These three are no longer to be trusted. They are to be under guard at all times and if any one of them attempt to escape, or to warn Deirdre once she is found, they are all to die. Is that clear?"

The look of complete shock on Moira's face brought a smile to Cathub's, the first since their arrival. "I see you understand at last, dear Moira. You three have served you purpose. You lent legitimacy to my venture. Your presence was important to keep Deirdre happy and unaware. You are no longer needed; therefore, do not try my patience further. I would as soon have Fedlimid's men deal with you now. I keep you alive only as insurance against any future need you might serve. But if you pose any danger to my plans, I will rid myself of you. All of you."

Doctors Cooper and Meaney, attracted by Cathub's raised voice, had heard the threat. Their shock mirrored Moira's and was only heightened by the ring of armed men that now closed about them.

"We must proceed, they only increase their head start on us as I waste my time with you three. Remember; cause me any further delay, if I have to even think of you again, I will leave your lifeless bodies by the path. Fedlimid let us continue."

It is well that Cathub did not realize that his order to have his three traveling companions under constant guard did actually slow their progress. They traveled without stopping, late into the evening. As night began to fall, they found themselves near a granite fall of stones that looked like a giants set of building blocks. There they spent a restless night. Cathub had them up early the next morning and on their way well before the sun had fully risen.

The constant rain seemed to have little effect on the Ulstermen. This was not the case for the time travelers. Unused to the heavy woolen cloaks and gown, the soaking rains seemed to drag them down. That and the sucking mud, the heavy foliage, as well as the menacing presence of the heavily armed Ulaid warriors dragged at their spirits as well as their bodies. They struggled to keep up, not wanting to draw down their former comrade's wrath upon them. Therefore, it was with great relief that they were able to sink to the ground when Fedlimid's tracker called them to a stop.

"Lord Cathub, there are tracks here. Down in the ravine. Small prints as though made by a woman. Recent they are, perhaps only just made the night past."

"How can you be sure they were made by the woman I seek?" Cathub asked of the man.

"They are made by the same shoe as those we found at the camp of the Eman Macha. There is something else. She travels alone, but another follows her."

"She has run from him, attempting to make her way back to me. Good girl, Deirdre, and your reward shall be marriage to the most powerful man in all of Eire... next to me, of course." The giggle that escaped from the old Druid was incongruous; did not fit with the image of power so carefully cultivated, and hinted at the madness that lurked there.

"Quickly, we return. Your guards will follow with the prisoners; the rest of us will make better time without them. They will meet us at the meadow. Quickly, Fedlimid, we must go now and travel through the night to make up for lost time. She is close and I will have her back."

# *Twelve*

*They come together*

A hand grasped Deirdre's shoulder, another closed over her mouth, cutting off the scream that surprise startled from her. Terror quickly gave way to relief, followed by consternation when she realized almost immediately that it was Niall. He had found her. How would she convince him that she needed desperately to find her friends?

The look on his face, and the finger brought up to his lips in the universal and timeless warning for silence, brought another emotion; wariness. Niall moved them quickly to the shelter of the dense forest undergrowth, careful to leave no trace of their passing. Mere moments had passed before Deirdre became aware of stealthy sounds around them. Movement, ever so slight, accompanied the sounds. She was aware that men were approaching the clearing by the rock fall that she and Niall had just vacated. A naturally curious soul, she leaned forward trying to see who it was that approached in such a clandestine manner, only to be pulled gently back by

Niall. A slight shake of his head made her realize the folly of her action. Nevertheless, it might be Dr. Daniels, Moira and the others who drew near.

In the next instance when she knew it was they, she also knew why Niall had sought a hiding place. It was Professor Daniels' voice she heard, but the words he spoke froze the greeting that had risen in her throat.

"By the gods, we have missed the bitch again! How am I ever to get Deirdre to her marriage to Conochar if she does not stay in one place long enough for me to get my hands on her? Have you found their track? Even I can see that the trail ends at the edge of this clearing, where have they gone?"

"My lord Cathub, we should head towards the meadow. It is certain the lady Deirdre would go there, do you not think?"

Deirdre's brow furrowed at the name Cathub, as she mouthed the word "who" to Niall, but he only held his finger to his lips and shook his head. They dared not move, as it was certain that one of Fedlimid's men would either see the motion or hear the movement. It was also certain that they could not stay as they were or the trackers were sure to come upon them, no matter how well hidden they might be.

Luck seemed to favor them, as someone shouted out from the other side of the clearing, "My lords, I have found tracks. They lead off this way." All moved toward the one who had called out, giving Niall the opportunity to draw Deirdre away quickly and quietly.

Once assured that they were well out of the range of hearing, Niall sat Deirdre upon a fallen tree and tried his best to explain.

"*Cailin*, I fear it is ill news I give you. As you heard, and I know from the look upon your face that you understood, deceitful plans have been laid against you by the hands of one you thought a friend. The Druid who arrived with you and your friends, who is known to me now as Cathub, has plotted to sell you into marriage with Conochar, High King of the Ulaid. This one will not care that you are already promised to me. This one considers you his possession already and will not hesitate to take you against your will. Naoisi brought this news to me that first night you spent in our camp, but I did not tell you, thinking it would only bring you pain, not knowing that you would go off into the forest on your own to find your companions."

This was a long speech for Niall and Deirdre had some difficulty following it, although she did understand what he was trying to tell her. Her skill with the language seemed to be improving. The point being, she understood the treachery Walter Daniels had plotted. A sudden thought occurred to her, "The others? What of them? Were they also involved in this plot?"

"No *Cailín*, they have been taken as prisoners by the Druid."

"I can not leave them under his power, can we not rescue them?"

"Just us two? No, little one, but I will send back men to attempt their rescue. We must hurry now. Run as much as possible, stop little, there is no time. I have left the horses some distance from here. They will soon discover that the track they follow, though it leads from the clearing to the meadow, is not a recent one and will conclude that we now head directly to my village." Bringing Deirdre to her feet, Niall urged her to haste, keeping as much as possible to the mossy areas that would not leave evidence of their passing.

"There will be no stopping this time, we must ride swiftly and through the night as well. They will be hard upon our trail all the way." The urgency in Niall's voice, as much as anything else, brought home to Deirdre the danger they were in.

"But Niall, there is an object that Walter has... I mean Cathub, which I must obtain. It is an amulet, which hangs about his neck on a heavy silver chain. It is in the form of a silver serpent coiled about a large crystal. I must have that crystal or all is lost for me... and my friends."

Within the amulet Deirdre spoke of lay hidden the triggering device that would return them to the twenty-second century, and therefore, it was her only means of escaping the horrendous scheme Walter Daniels had plotted against her. The shock of this revelation threatened to shut down her thought processes. Only Niall's constant urging kept her thoughts from blanking out altogether. How could she deal with such deception, such corrupt behavior? She could not help but wonder how long this plot had been in the making. Had he chosen her for this adventure with this marriage in mind? Or did it go further back than that?

Walter Daniels had been a close friend of her parents. It was he who had instilled a love of the ancient Celtic societies in Deirdre and had urged her to study the ways of the Celt. His stories of his native Ireland had held the young Deirdre's imagination like nothing else. Deirdre had always assumed that it was for this reason he had offered this seemingly marvelous opportunity. It was obvious now that it was only in order to prepare her for the life he'd had in mind for her, that he might sell her to this Conochar. Was it possible that he had concocted this evil plot so many years ago?

"I will get this charm for you. Once I have you safely hidden with my own people, I will lead the warriors who will rescue your people. These are your family?"

"No, not family, just very dear friends. My parents were killed three years ago. Walter, I mean Cathub, had been a friend of theirs and stepped in to help me cope with their death. Two years ago, he offered to include me in this adventure; to visit your country and learn the ways of your people. He told me that he had made at least three other visits previously. That must have been when he concocted this awful deception."

Out of breath from running and talking at the same time, Deirdre stopped. "I have to catch my breath, Niall. I can't go on much further."

Slumping against a nearby tree, Deirdre felt compelled to explain the close relationship she had developed with her companions.

"Moira became a substitute mother. In fact, truth be told, she is much more of a mother to me than my own was. My mother and father were very involved in their careers, and had little time for a child. Dr. Meaney and Dr. Collins became the uncles I never had. So, yes, I guess you could say that they are my family, or the closest thing to a family I am likely to have."

"But, *Cailín*, you have a very large family now. My sons, Naoisi, Ardan and Ilam, my daughter Levarcham, Ardan's wife, who will have a child soon, all are now your family. I have three brothers, all with wives and children. All of my kin and clansmen will welcome you into the clan as one of our own. As my wife, you will never be without kinsmen to protect and provide for you."

Without warning, Niall froze in his tracks, placing a hand around Deirdre's arm. Signaling for silence, he once again drew her into the camouflage of the forest; his hand touched the hilt of the sword at his side. Deirdre did not know what had caused this sudden caution, but knew by now to follow as Niall led if she was to avoid the dangers of this world. She soon found out the reason for Niall's caution as the sounds of the forest began to change. She found that the longer she inhabited this world, the easier it became to read it. The whispering sounds of the forest foliage changed subtly, men moved through the forest disturbing the sounds inherent there. A twig snapped, clothing rustled against foliage.

Deirdre's wariness quickly turned to surprise. As suddenly as had been Niall's plunge into hiding, he just as suddenly stepped from their hidey-hole, bringing Deirdre with him. Naoisi, Ardan and several other men emerged from the forest.

"We found your horse, Da, and left ours with Bal. Two men guard them. When you did not return to the village, we came looking for you, and found both sets of tracks heading back here. We thought you might need some help, yes?" Looking slightly abashed, Naoisi continued, "And I could not have my new mother lost when you have only just found her, could I then?"

"You have the instincts that will make a great leader for our people, Naoisi. Your face is most welcome just now, and I am proud to call myself your sire. Fedlimid, the Druid Cathub, and Conochar's warriors will be following soon, if they have not already discovered that they follow an old track. Take Deirdre back to the village, I will take these men and attempt to rescue her family from her enemies."

"I do not wish to question your orders, Da," Ardan spoke. "Would it not be best if all returned to the village. Men can be posted along the way, watching for the opportunity to rescue these new kin of ours from the clutches of this Druid Cathub, and Fedlimid. These woods afford many an opportunity to pick off stragglers one at a time without alerting others. I would enjoy seeing the look upon this evil priest's face when he discovers that his prisoners have been snatched from beneath his nose."

"A good plan, my son. I can see that all my seeds have grown well." They had been speaking while moving otherwise silently through the forest. Now, having reached their horses, all mounted and, without further discussion, set out for the west.

# *Thirteen*

## *The Village*

They rode hard through the night. Deirdre thought she would never be able to look at a horse the same way again. "Parts of my body hurt that I never even knew existed on my body," she said to herself.

The countryside was breathtaking, but Deirdre was bone weary from three days of walking and riding through the woodlands of Ireland. She thought she must have dozed off several times, but never for long. The pace Niall and his men maintained did not lend itself well to sleep. Deirdre rode behind Niall, which required that she maintain a firm grip around his waist in order to keep from slipping from the horses back. Although, she did not believe he would have allowed that to happen. More than once she felt his large hand close over her own that gripped, knuckles white with the strain, the girdle that belted his leather tunic.

Around dawn, the riders left the wooded area and came out into open territory. Deirdre's escort of warriors quickly became much more wary now that they had left the cover of the forest; watching for those who certainly must be following.

Not long after, their party reached a great lake, turned and began to travel northward along the lakeshore. The pace was numbing although the travel was easier at this point; they now had a well-used path to follow. The lake narrowed into a swiftly moving waterway before it once again widened into another, much larger lake. Soon she began to see the signs of civilization. Everywhere there were tiny stone raths with wattle fences, cultivated fields, and they began to meet people along the way who called out as their party passed by. Everyone they met along the road was warned of the possibility that Conochar's warriors may well be close on their trail.

Niall explained, "These are my clansmen and though they do not live within the village, they are still of my clan, pay allegiance to me and expect my protection."

The signs of civilization became more and more pronounced until at last they came to Niall's village. Scattered about were many small circular huts with conical, thatched roofs that reached nearly to the ground. A low wattle fence encircled each, which appeared to be more effective at keeping in livestock and toddlers, than it would be in keeping out invaders.

The main compound of the village seemed much more defensible; consisting of a cut-stone wall that appeared to be approximately twelve to fifteen feet high, topped by sharpened timber thrust into the top of the stone wall, creating a solid barrier of hardwood, and adding an additional five feet. A man could stand upon the top of the stone wall, protected by the timber and defend his people. A single gate allowed entrance to the compound within, which contained several small stone structures such as those Deirdre had noticed as they approached. This was a relatively well-fortified community.

Deirdre realized then that she had been hearing about these compounds since arriving in Ireland; a ring-fort they were called. Extremely defensible and well constructed, there were still remnants of over forty thousand ring-forts to be found in contemporary Ireland; albeit none were much more than archeological digs.

Niall's youngest son Ilam, and his only surviving daughter Levarcham, met Niall and Deirdre at the gate. The boy nodded to Deirdre with a reserved courtesy and, taking the horse's lead from his father, left without a word. Levarcham, however, was full of curiosity. Her questions rained down upon both of them.

"Are you to be my new mother now? Where did you come from? Is your country very far from here? Is it true what they say, you can make yourself appear and disappear from out of the air? I am to be betrothed to Máirtín of the *Hy Drona* at the next gathering, am I not, Da? It will be very good for our people and Máirtín is to be Chieftain of his people. He is very handsome."

They walked as Levarcham chatted. Niall led them toward the center of the compound where there stood a much larger version of the odd circular, thatched, stone huts. This one was large enough, according to Niall, to accommodate all of his extended clan in the event of an emergency or invasion. It looked to Deirdre that it would be a very tight fit.

"Beneath the Great Hall," Niall explained, "there is a souterrain, a hole dug into the floor, which is reached by way of a ladder, and leads to an underground room for food storage and a passage to be used as emergency escape. The tunnel leads under the stone wall and opens out into a heavily wooded area located very near the lake edge. In the event Fedlimid's men should break through the village defenses, you are to use this escape route and hide yourself until I come for you."

"Do you really think Cathub will attack the village?"

There was a sense of peace here. The compound was alive with children; Niall's brothers and their families each dwelt within the stone walls, as did Niall himself, with his sons and daughter. The air was fragrant with rhododendron, fuchsia and a variety of orchids left by the passing of a glacier several thousands years before. Contentment seemed to wash over her as Niall and his daughter, this sweet child who had very quickly attached herself to Deirdre, led her around their home. It was inconceivable to her that she should be the cause of any harm coming to these people.

"Aye, he will. It is only a matter of time."

"Niall, there must be another way. I cannot allow your people to suffer because of me. If you could just get Cathub's amulet for me, I can make all of this go away.

Once I have the amulet, Cathub will know I am beyond his reach."

"You must trust me. Conochar will not give you up. Cathub may know you to be out of his reach, but Conochar will not relinquish you without a fight. Enough of this for now."

The area encompassed by the stone enclosure was quite large; containing small, thatched stone structures intended for the storage of feed for their animals, weapons and building materials, as well as four family homes, one for each of Niall's brothers and their families, Ardan and his wife, and of course the home of Niall and those of his children that still remained under his roof. Deirdre began to wonder where she would fit into this well ordered family unit, but Niall seemed to read her mind.

"*Cailín*," this time he did not use the term of affection to address Deirdre, but Levarcham, "let us take our Deirdre and show her to the visitor's lodgings in the Great Hall." Pointing to the largest structure in the compound, which she had correctly assumed to be the community gathering place, Levarcham took Deirdre's hand and led her off. Head held high, his chest puffed out, Niall swaggered behind his women.

It was a very large structure, at least sixty-five feet in diameter, and was much more comfortable than she had expected. The floor had been flagged with the beautiful green stone known in Deirdre's time as Connemara Marble and sweet smelling rushes had been recently strewn about the floor. There were no separate rooms but one very large open area, with a granite hearth sitting low and squat in the middle of the open dwelling. There was no flue, but it was not needed, the head high stone walls, combined with the conical shape of the thatched roof, allowed a gentle upward draft to enter. The room was kept warm and comfortable, while the smoke from the hearth was drawn naturally upward on the heated air to the small hole at the top of the roof, some fifteen feet or more above her head. A loft, located about eight feet off the ground, ran three-quarters of the way around the structure. Deirdre assumed that this was where guests were bedded down, and where Niall's people would live during a siege of the village. Ladders firmly attached at intervals around the room reached the loft. The area under the loft had been fitted with low benches and tables. It seemed that this structure was also used for gatherings; festivals, weddings, and other celebrations perhaps.

"Deirdre, I've asked the wives of my brothers to help you to get settled. You will need clothing and other woman's things." He reddened at that last. "Niambh will be along soon. She will be putting together a gown for you to be wed properly. You are to consider this place your own home until you come to me as my wife, and my home becomes yours."

Deirdre could only wonder at the confused look on Levarcham's face as she stared at her father. Was the girl concerned about Deirdre becoming her father's wife? Was she jealous of sharing her father with another woman? Deirdre could have quieted the child's fears simply by letting her know that she could not possibly go through with marrying Niall.

"We will leave you now to settle. Niambh will join you shortly. And I shall check in on you later." This last was said with a look that promised more than just a casual visit. "Come, Levie."

"Settle in." Deirdre's cheerful mood left her even as Niall and his daughter did. "What have I to do to settle in? I don't have any possessions to unpack. No clothing save what I have on my back." Though Deirdre spoke these words out loud, she spoke them to herself, therefore, when they were answered, she nearly jumped out of her skin.

"Well, it's a good thing I've come then, isn't it?" The woman who stood in the doorway was tall, had a well-proportioned and comfortable frame, and was probably in her mid to late twenties. In spite of her relative youth, long rusty-red hair plaited down her back was liberally threaded with silver. Life was hard in this world and youth did not last long. The woman's face reflected the humor of her words, and it appeared that this was a natural look for her.

Deirdre thought, *I shall like this woman I think.*

"So, Deirdre is it? I am Niambh, in case you haven't figured that out for yourself. So, you've captured our elusive chieftain, have you? Many have tried, none have succeeded, 'til now." Her eyes twinkled in a very unsubtle manner. "There will be plenty who will sulk; but they'll recover. These are good people here.

“Is it true you appeared to the men from out of the sky? Did you float down from above, or just appear from nowhere? Are you a Druid priestess then?

“It was a sad business when our Niall lost his dear Fionna to the childbed. We all thought he would never recover.” She tsked.

“Already people are in a wonder at the change what has come over our Niall. Sullen as an old sow, he was. From the day his Fionna passed until... well, until he met you it would seem. None thought he would ever take another wife.”

Perhaps that explained the curious look on Levarcham’s face. Her father was a changed man, and it seemed that she, Deirdre, had much to do with the transformation.

“And here you are, about to become his wife. I’m told that you’ve run from a forced marriage... to Conochar. Well, you’ve good judgment if you’ve chosen our Niall over that one.”

Deirdre was beginning this think this woman was the source of all information in this village. Perhaps Niall had sent her to Deirdre for that very purpose.

“They say he’s in league with evil forces,” she whispered, and laid a finger up against the side of her nose. Deirdre wasn’t quite sure what that gesture meant, but could imagine it wasn’t good.

*Evil forces. That would be Cathub. How much more evil could one person get?*

"Let's get you out of that gown and into something clean. Will you have a wash first? Let me just go fetch some hot water." With that, she was out the door. Deirdre realized that she had not asked a single question, nor said a single word, and yet had learned a great deal.

Sitting upon a nearby bench, Deirdre struggled to regroup. She had discovered that her trusted surrogate father had not only betrayed her, but had done so in a particularly spectacular way. She had become affianced to the barbarian prince of a minor tribe in ancient Celtic Ireland, was thought to be a Druid priestess with magical powers. And, oh yes, was in hiding from the High King of a much more powerful tribe, who thought he owned her body and soul, and wished to force her into the unwanted marriage. And now she had put these good people in jeopardy merely through her presence in their village. *Way to go, Deirdre, not bad for a few days work!*

Suddenly it was just too much. After four very trying days, her emotions were on a roller-coaster ride since arriving in the past and her thoughts were in extreme turmoil. She began to shake uncontrollably. Wrapping her arms protectively about herself, Deirdre tried unsuccessfully to control the violent shaking. Then came the tears, accompanied by great gasping sobs.

"I can't do this anymore," she sobbed, "how... how... how can I go on like this?"

When Niambh returned, she found Deirdre on the verge of hysteria. Pulling her close and wrapping her arms around the frenzied girl, Niambh settled herself on the bench beside Deirdre and began to rock her slowly, cooing softly, murmuring meaningless but comforting words. She waved away the curious who came to the door to see what the fuss was about. Deirdre buried her face in Niambh's shoulder, and poured out her sorrows, most of which was unintelligible. Slowly the hysteria began to fade.

"There's our brave girl. Our Niall will make it all better. Just you wait and see." Peering into the girl's tear reddened face, Niambh seemed satisfied with what she saw there. "All better now? Let's get you washed up and into bed. A good cry can be a healing thing, but it's food and a good night's sleep you'll be needing most right now."

With the efficiency of an experienced wife and mother, Niambh quickly had Deirdre out of her soiled garments and into a bronze tub that had quickly and quietly arrived and been filled with warm water by unseen hands while Niambh had been busy comforting Deirdre. While she was being soaped and lathered, the word was just as quickly and quietly being spread throughout the village that the sorceress called Deirdre, whom the returning warriors had already been telling tales of, and whom the entire village was whispering about, was actually just a very frightened and exhausted young woman. Unbeknownst to Deirdre, her fit of tears had done more to endear her to Niall's people than anything she could have purposely attempted.

"We will be burying our men on the morrow. You will accompany our Niall then?"

Startled, Deirdre realized it was barely a few days since the battle she had quite literally landed in the middle of, and of course those who had died would require the ritual of burial. "Yes, of course. It will be my honor to be included in the ceremony."

"Then you had best eat something and right to bed with you."

The succulent smell of lamb stew wafted through the air from the small table nearest the door. Some other unseen helper had stolen in quietly, deposited the meal and left without a sound. Drawn to the delectable aroma, Deirdre, not bothering to dress, dragged a woolen blanket about her shoulders, sat herself down and began to wolf down the rich, gravy laden stew.

"This is wonderful," she exclaimed around a mouth full of stew. "I hadn't realized just how hungry I was until I smelled this mouthwatering stew." Laughing, Deirdre used the tip of her tongue to capture the dribble of gravy that threatened to run down her chin from the corner of her mouth.

Satisfied that her charge was well on the way to recovery, Niambh gave Deirdre final orders to finish everything on the table before her and, when done, to retire to the bed in the loft above. Niambh patted her shoulder with affection, then left her to her meal. Although only a few years older than her, Deirdre felt as though she had just been adopted by this motherly, kind woman.

Clean, satisfied, and with her appetite finally sated, Deirdre found she could not keep her eyes open one minute longer. Wrapping the blanket about her, she managed to negotiate the sturdy ladder leading to bed and sleep. Her eyes closed and sleep overtook her even as her head touched the soft fur-covered pallet—the sounds of children playing, and the life of the village going on around her, lulled her even deeper into welcome oblivion.

Well after night had fallen and the village had gone silent for the night, Deirdre fought her way up from the panic of nightmarish visions. She did not, at first, recognize her surroundings. Slowly, it came to her where she was, and she became aware that she was not alone. Not frightened, she knew instinctively whom it was that watched her from the night-darkened shadows. *Niall!* Her breath caught in her chest, the beat of her heart quickened, and a very pleasant tingle began between her thighs.

"Niall," She whispered into the darkness. She could not keep a small note of fear from creeping into her heart. "Is it the Ulaid? Has Cathub come to attack the village?"

"No, *Cailín*, Cathub and the Ulaid have taken up camp several hours march from here. He has not molested the people and appears to be gathering his courage to attack. I have men who report their every movement watching their camp. We will be informed well in advance of any attack.

Reassured, Deirdre's initial desire for Niall returned with forceful urgency. "Then why do you sit there, alone among the shadows?"

"You slept so peacefully, I did not wish to wake you. Only just before you woke did I realize the night terrors were upon you, and I moved to awaken you."

"That is very considerate of you." There was a definite teasing tone to her voice now. "But there is no need to sit there in the corner by yourself now that I am awake." Rising to her knees upon the fur covered pallet, Deirdre allowed the blanket that had covered her to slip away, leaving her naked before the man that so easily quickened her pulse and weakened her knees. "Come here to me, Niall."

"Ah, woman. Seeing you rise from your bed, unclothed, to greet me, to command me to your bed, how can I not obey?" Shedding tunic and braecs Niall came to her. The impact of their bodies meeting lifted Deirdre from her kneeling position to land flat upon her back, Niall firmly atop her, her legs wrapped about his waist.

"Watching you sleep has brought me peace, but seeing you thus makes my blood burn." His hands were everywhere upon her trembling body. His mouth seared her flesh; his tongue lashed her breasts bringing her fully erect nipples to a diamond hard state that would have cut glass. Searching, tasting, exploring, Niall took possession of her, and Deirdre gave herself to him willingly.

Hours later, Deirdre woke to a feeling of utter and total contentment. Niall slept soundly beside her. This was the second time she had awoken next to this man who was in reality a virtual stranger. But deep within, she knew he had become a necessary part of her being. Looking at him brought her such peace and yet stirred in her a wild passion previously unknown to her. How could she possibly leave him? To return to what; a world that worshiped science, but distained the humanities, a world where DNA and the Human Genome were sacred cows, yet the study of art, literature, and music were ridiculed as wasted time?

Niall stirred, stretched and growled contentedly, yet continued to sleep. Dawn was still hours away. Deirdre looked upon him. His body was scarred, but beautiful. Not the slender, youthful body of a young man, but the work hardened, sculpted body of a mature man. His chest was wide and deep, lifting and falling with each breath taken in and released. Softly furred; rusty-red down covered the chiseled, muscular abdomen, damply curled about his navel, narrowed and vee'd, then arrowed down between thighs of hardened oak. Not an ounce of fat was evident anywhere upon his body. His arms were steel bands; she knew them well, for they had held her tightly through out the night. Strong, unyielding, yet tender enough to hold her gently, to offer protection and comfort. She asked herself once again; how could she leave him? And yet she knew she must. This was not her time and she did not belong here. But if that were so, why did it feel so right?

Unconsciously, Deirdre reached out and began to stroke the downy fur covering Niall's rock hard belly.

Although he was not yet awake, his body reacted to her touch instantaneously. Delighted, Deirdre continued to stroke, watching Niall's arousal grow and harden.

# *Fourteen*

## *Preparation for Siege*

It had taken too long to discover the trail they followed was in fact many days old. Cathub would not admit, even to himself, that he was largely to blame. It was *not* his fault. In his feverish rush to lay his hands on Deirdre, the key to his path to wealth and power, Cathub had ordered Fedlimid and his men to rush headlong back to the site of the battle, the place where the time-travelers had thrust themselves into this time period. The pace they set left little time for the trackers to study the trail they followed; he, Cathub knew where it led. Deirdre was attempting to return to him. It was that barbarian who continually thwarted his plans and kept Deirdre from him.

Too late, it was discovered that the trail they followed was an old one. Too late, Cathub realized that ordering the death of the two trackers for failing to realize the trail was stale was not a wise move. This whittled the number of men who followed him down to eight, a very small army of warriors. Too late, he recognized the wisdom of

Fedlimid's recommendation to send to Conochar for additional men.

It wasn't his fault; the men who surrounded him were incompetent. How could he be expected to carry out Deirdre's return if he could not depend upon his advisers? Fedlimid should have told his men to check the trail more carefully. Fedlimid should have insisted upon sending to Conochar for additional men. Fedlimid should have warned him that the deaths of those two trackers would greatly reduce their numbers. Yes, it was Fedlimid's fault, as well as the fault of that barbarian chieftain, Niall.

"My lord, this place will make a good encampment," Fedlimid interrupted Cathub's musings. Dismounting, he contemplated the area chosen by Conochar's man.

"Am I to sleep upon the ground yet again, Fedlimid?" Even Cathub recognized the wheedling tones of a querulous old man. Clearing his throat, he began again.

"You will find a suitable accommodation where I will be sheltered. Throw the inhabitants out, or kill them, whatever you must do. We are too far into Eman Macha territory now, and I must have the protection of stone about me. This Niall could creep up on us while we sleep, cut our throats and have Deirdre to himself without so much as a skirmish."

"If you will note, my lord, there is a stone rath just there. It appears the people of Clan Eman Macha have been made aware of our approach as the dwelling has been voluntarily vacated."

"Very well, Fedlimid. Settle your men in. We will abide here until Conochar sends us more men. You may sleep at the entrance to the cottage to protect me, and your men will keep guard through the night. Bring food to me there when it has been prepared." Swirling his robes about him, Cathub proceeded to the small thatched hut that, from a distance, had looked more like a stack of hay surrounded by a fence of woven sticks than a dwelling.

They would remain here until Cathub was certain he would possess the upper hand. He would not approach the Eman Macha village without the certainty of superior numbers. Cathub had witnessed first hand the skill with which his enemy could fight, and the Ulaid were seriously outnumbered. It would not do to endanger himself unnecessarily.

Conochar would send more warriors. Once he, Cathub, had wrested Deirdre from the clutches of Niall of the Eman Macha, he would have the village put to death for daring to defy the great Druid Cathub. Deirdre would witness the destruction of her captors and she would be grateful. Perhaps he would burn down the village with all of them still in it! Once Deirdre realized the extent to which he would go to protect her and ensure her safety, she would realize that he only had her best interest at heart. She would accept her marriage to Conochar as a good match.

After all, what reasons did she have to return to the twenty-second century? She would be alone, without family or friends. Her skills, her education, were in a field that was all but extinct. She would have no money, no career and no one to care for her. He had made sure of all this years ago. It was he who had guided Deirdre into the study of ancient cultures, specifically the Celtic societies of Ancient Ireland. It was he who had removed her parents from the scene when they had begun to question his plans for *their* girl. How dare they refer to Deirdre as their girl, when it was clear that Deirdre belonged to Cathub from the beginning?

Was it not he who had brought the child to them to adopt? Was it not he, Cathub, who had given them the money to raise and educate the child? One would think they had loved and wanted the child from the beginning, when he'd had to bribe them with grants so that they might continue their research, before they would even consider taking Deirdre and raising her as their own. In the end they had claimed to love and cherish Deirdre as their own. They had threatened to tell her all. They had dared to threaten *Cathub*.

Killing them had been easy. He was a physicist. He had any number of weapons at his disposal, weapons that left no trace. He had simply used one of them to disable their vehicle, allowing them to plunge over an embankment... no more parental problems.

"My lord, your meal has been prepared." Once again, Fedlimid's voice interrupted Cathub's thoughts.

"My lord, the messenger we sent will not reach Lord Conochar until tomorrow at the earliest. It will take two full days for them to arrive here. We should discuss plans for the siege now, my lord, so that we will be ready to proceed when Conochar's men arrive."

"Plans? The plan is simple. We will surround their pathetic little village. If they refuse to give Deirdre to me, we will lay waste to their homes and crops, kill their cattle, and if all else fails, burn down their village around their ears. That is my plan."

"My lord, my men tell me the people have already abandoned their homes and taken their food and cattle with them. There isn't so much as a chicken left, and these simple stone huts can be easily rebuilt. These threats will not move the Eman Macha."

"Do you defy me, Fedlimid? My plan is set. We will move as soon as Conochar's men arrive."

# *Fifteen*

*a ghrá mo chroí*

Her scent was still strong. She had not abandoned him during the night as she had done before. That honeyed scent Niall had, from the beginning, associated with Deirdre, still lingered on his body, on the blankets that he lay upon, and most important, it still hung in the air he breathed.

While he feigned sleep, Niall's body awoke to Deirdre's caressing fingers, touching, exploring tentatively, and bringing him to full arousal. Niall allowed Deirdre to explore his body, stomach muscles clenched as her wet tongue dipped into his belly button, then trailed wet tongue-trails upwards where straight white teeth nipped gently at rock hard nipples. Soft, her silken hands caressed, while her hot wet tongue lapped and teased, and Niall could feign sleep no longer.

Grabbing Deirdre's arms, Niall pulled her to him then rolled over to trap her beneath him. "Stop, *Cailín*, we must speak of what is to come, and I cannot think while you touch me thus." Niall rolled Deirdre around so that her bottom fitted snugly against his swollen member, while he tried with only partial success to will his painful erection into a more manageable state.

"Niambh will come soon to help you prepare for the burial ceremony. You will accompany me? It is what is expected of the Chieftain's wife."

"Niambh and I have already discussed this, Niall. Of course I will accompany you. What is it that is really on your mind? Is it Cathub?"

"Cathub does not worry me. He is an evil old man, but his senses leave him. The men who watch the Ulaid encampment report that the old Druid speaks to himself, that he is not right in his head. It is Conochar that I fear. If he decides to accompany his warriors, to take charge of the siege himself, I fear we will have little chance against him. We must form a plan for your escape in the event the village falls to Conochar's forces."

"Escape, without you, without the villagers? No I will stay here with you."

"Those are brave words, but I will not take the chance of you falling into Conochar's grasp."

Resting his cheek against hers, Niall felt the thrumming of blood as it coursed through the veins in his neck, or was it the blood in her veins he felt there where their two necks touched? He whispered, "Sleep, *a ghrá mo chroí*, love of my heart. Morning comes swiftly. We will speak of this again."

# *Sixteen*

## *Isle of the dead*

Niambh came to them early, while night still darkened the coming day and long before the light of dawn would awaken the rest of the occupants of the village, bringing with her appropriate garb for Deirdre to wear to the burial ceremony.

She shooed Niall from the Great Hall, and helped Deirdre to dress. The gown, which fitted Deirdre like a second skin, was of very soft, finely woven wool dyed a deep, vibrant blue. Over that, Niambh pulled a loosely fitted tunic of fine doeskin, worked to the suppleness of chamois. Decorative designs of interwoven knots had been embroidered around the neck and hem. A necklace of amber beads and bronze disks was hung about Deirdre's neck, with a matching girdle clasped about her waist. Finishing, Niambh pulled a sheer veil, which matched the blue of Deirdre's gown, from her cache of finery, draped it over Deirdre's hair and settled it into place with a circlet of intricately worked bronze.

It was still fully dark when Niall met her at the entrance to the hut, took her hand in his, and together they led the people of the Eman Macha down to the lakeshore; the lowering moon lighting their path. There, a small armada of little *curragh* awaited Clan Eman Macha and the warriors who waited patiently to be sent on to the Other World.

Mist formed and rose from the lake's surface, curling about the small watercraft, then rising to swirl and play about the small boat. The silver disk of the full moon hung heavy and low on the western horizon.

The journey was not a hurried one. They rowed past one island after another. The first was quite large, with low rounded hills, green with waving, waist high grasses. Deirdre watched the coastline with interest as they rowed past. It appeared to be uninhabited.

After approximately an hour spent riding the waters of the lake and just as the first light of dawn reddened the eastern sky, their boat finally arrived at a tiny, inconspicuous little island. Boa, it was called. The other *curragh* followed them closely.

Boa was fringed with small trees and low growing fern. A cut-stone jetty jutted out into the waters of the lake, allowing the small craft a place to moor. Niall handed Deirdre from the *curragh*, then led her to the stone dais at the foot of the jetty. There they waited as Niall's people arrived and assembled. Two wizened old men in the robes of the Druid were already in place on the dais. The ceremony would not begin until all were present. Only a handful of the Eman Macha warriors had remained behind to protect the village from attack.

Without a word or obvious signal, the two old priests turned as one and, signaling to Niall to follow, began the trek that would lead them along a time worn, stone path, winding its way up the side of a low lying rise. It was not really even a hill, perhaps six or seven feet maybe slightly more; the sides were not steep. As they neared the top, Deirdre began to suspect that this was not a naturally occurring hillock. Her suspicion was confirmed when they reached the top of the rise. It was, in fact, perfectly round and flat-topped, with a shallow, bowl-like area in the middle. Deirdre realized that it looked like a very ancient ring-fort that had been overtaken by nature. Very much like those archeological sites she had visited in her own time.

The top of the hillock was perhaps eight feet wide, paved with flagstone with stone paths leading down into the arena-like area below. At one end, a cave-like entrance, faced and supported with decorated stone, led back into the bowels of the structure, and most likely tunneled around the sides.

Once she and Niall had reached the stone paved area over the cave entrance, and the people of the Eman Macha had ringed the hilltop, the elder of the two priests stepped forward, calling the people to attention. The younger of the priests began to make his way down a stony path to the arena below.

"Niall, how long have your people used this site for their burials?" Unable to contain her curiosity any longer, Deirdre just had to ask.

"The Druids began bringing my people here during the time of my Great Grandsire. They tell us that this was the dwelling place of the *Tuatha de Danaan,* the children of the goddess Danaan, in that time when they inhabited the earth."

A clearing of the throat and a pointed look from one of the Druids had them both feeling like chastened children. A very inappropriate giggle threatened to escape from Deirdre's throat.

Only then did Deirdre cast her attention to the ritual site, a grassy area strewn with Blue Bells, Bells of Ireland and an array of other wildflowers, making the area look like nothing more than a woodland meadow. Belying that impression, Deirdre spotted two stone figures; one smaller and obviously older than the other to one side of the cave entrance. Both appeared to have inhabited this site for many years, long into the past. The larger of the stones was what would later come to be known as a Janus stone because the figure had two faces, as did the Roman god Janus. As the god of doors and gates, Janus was also thought to represent new beginnings, as in rebirth, and was therefore often found in ancient burial sites. But this figure was not Roman, it appeared to be much more ancient.

Deirdre also noticed that the grounds were uneven and liberally dotted with ancient, ornately carved stones—burial stones.

Four shallow, freshly dug round holes scarred what was otherwise a peaceful, pastoral scene. This would be the final resting place of those men whose deaths Deirdre had witnessed just a hand-full of days past. In each grave, Deirdre saw, through the quickly gathering light, personal items evidently meant to ease the fallen warriors path into the Otherworld. In one she noted a bronze pike, stone celt, pewter bowl, and a leather pouch containing objects known only to the man's loved ones. In another, Deirdre could just make out four wooden wheels and a wooden platform; a dismantled wagon perhaps, along with two stone jars and a bronze sword gleaming with a dull light. The other two graves were too far away and the light too dim to make out what objects lay within.

Deirdre realized that while her attention had been elsewhere, she had all but missed the ritual incantation the Druid had been intoning. With a flourish of staff, the Druid called to the families of the fallen to bring their loved ones forth. From the four points of the compass, four parties of warriors bearing their departed upon broad shoulders detached themselves from the onlookers and made their way down the side of the hill, each taking up positions beside a freshly dug grave. The mists of the lake, drawn by the coming light of dawn, began to snake its way in and around the ancient burial grounds.

The old priest's voice rose and the sound swelled upon the early dawn air.

"In this sacred place, in the name of our fallen warriors, we call for the many blessing of our Lady of the Moon, whose aspect speaks to us from the elemental west." The Druid pointed his staff at the setting moon just visible on the western horizon, across the placid waters of the lake. "And those of the Green Man, Lord of the Wild Places, who even now rises from his place of rest in the east." Again pointing with his staff, this time in the general direction of the rising sun. "The Wheel of Life turns. All things are born, die and are born again. Our warriors have gone forth into the next phase of their journey. We mourn their passing and yet rejoice in their journey. The body they leave behind is but an empty house. We return it to the earth, the body of the Mother, from whom all are born."

The sociologist in Deirdre had come alive. Here was an actual Druid burial ceremony. There was no written language from this era; so none of this had survived into modern time. This ceremony had not been witnessed in almost two thousand years.

Her attention riveted to the scene below, her eye caught the slightest of movement at the mouth of the cave. A tiny wizened figure emerged. Dressed in black garments of rags, with a black veil hiding her head and face, Deirdre recognized the figure as the crone aspect of the Triple Goddess. The *Cailleach* or death hag. Normally associated with war and battles, it was nevertheless the *Cailleach* who would guide the souls of the dead warriors through the portal leading to the Other World.

The crone approached the first of the dead and circled about the prone figure. The pallbearers, having drawn back at the crone's approach, now turned and moved quickly up the side of the hill, returning to the relative safety of the crowd.

Thrice the crone circled the fallen warrior. She stopped and held her hand claw-like before her. She plunged her hand and arm into the chest of the dead man. Pulling her arm back, dripping with blood, she held aloft a black object, which writhed in her hand. Opening her fingers, to the cheers of the crowd, she released a large black raven into the sky.

The soul of the departed was now free of its physical body, free now to be led into the Other World, where he could be reborn.

Each of the dead was, in turn, treated to the same ceremonial liberation of their soul. The old woman, having uttered not a word throughout the ceremony, turned and re-entered the maw of the cave. To the amazement of all, including Deirdre, the four ravens, which had wheeled and circled above the ritual site, now turned as one and followed the old priestess into the mouth of the cavern.

Once the crone had gone, the kin of each of the dead came down to the burial grounds, placed the body of their dead warrior into the final resting place so carefully prepared for them, and lifted the burial stone into place over their departed. Garlands adorned with apples were placed upon the graves; symbols of both death and eternal life.

The voyage back to the village held none of the solemnity that had shrouded their earlier trip to the island. Neighbors chatted back and forth between the tiny vessels. Details of the evening's festivities were discussed. Now that the rituals had been observed, the dead warriors would be toasted into the Other World. Stories would be told, drinking horns raised, and entertainment would abound.

## *Seventeen*

*Journal Entry*
*Deirdre*

*It has been several days since I last opened this journal and put pen to paper. Much has happened. Professor Walter Daniels, who now calls himself Cathub, Druid Priest, the man I had come to look upon as a substitute for my parents, has been revealed to be not only treacherous, but is now to be viewed as a deadly enemy, bent upon selling me into marriage for his own gain.*

*I do not know how I should be feeling about this, but mostly I alternate between rage, and numbness.*

*My feelings for Niall continue to grow. I do not know how I will find the strength to leave him, but I know that I must. I do not belong here, although this place and these people become more and more dear to me every minute I spend with them. Niambh has become more than just a future sister-in-law to me, she has become a dear friend. At one point during the celebration that followed the burial ceremony, we both found ourselves seeking the relative quiet of a darkened corner of the Great Hall. We talked together for sometime, sharing a horn of ale. I found out much about Niall's youth, his dead wife, and his children. I learned how he had suffered with the loss of two children during childbirth and how the last had cost him his wife, Fionna. Another reason to berate myself for the way I have handled things since my arrival. With my leaving, this man will suffer one more loss, or do I overestimate his feelings for me? Niambh told me that his people had encouraged him to take another wife; perhaps I am just a convenient replacement.*

*Niall and Naoisi seem to have reconciled their differences, whatever they might have been. That also happened during last night's celebration for the dead. Naoisi had returned from his observations of Cathub's encampment to report their activities. He and Niall shunned the drinking and carousing, and found a quiet corner of the compound away from the festivities, and talked well into the night. Father and son, they are so alike. It made my heart lighten to see them sitting together, elbows on knees, heads bowed in deep conversation, at one point, laughing at some story.*

*The revelry went on well into the early hours. My bed being located in the loft above all the activity, it was well on to dawn before I was able seek it out and sleep. I thought Niall would seek me out at some point during the wee hours, but morning found my bed occupied by myself alone.*

*I did find him below, sitting at one of the tables with a breakfast feast spread before him. His grin could only have been in response to the way I had immediately tucked into that banquet. If nothing else, this place has been very good for my appetite.*

*That was this morning. I sit now upon a low bench just outside the Great Hall, enjoying the sun.*

*Children play in the compound around me. One in particular, a small girl of around three, seems to have attached herself to me. She fell while trying to follow the older children in play, skinned her knee, then came and buried her tear-streaked face in the skirt of my gown. After I had comforted her, rocking the small form in my lap, and kissed the injured knee to make it feel better, she fell asleep. The child's mother, my dear new friend Niambh, has taken her into their dwelling for her nap. My lap feels empty, my arms are empty. I wonder what it would feel like to hold Niall's child in my arms?*

*Levie has spent much of the day sitting here with me. She is a wonderful child, although I can hardly call her a child, considering she is to be promised in marriage this coming spring when the tribes gather. She speaks of nothing else, and I understand Niambh is helping her to put together a trousseau of wedding clothes.*

*Ardan's very pregnant wife has also visited me. She is a delightfully rosy girl who has kept me entertained with humorous stories about one villager after another. Stories I am sure the villager in question would rather not be recounted.*

*I have also had the opportunity to get to know Niall's youngest son, Ilam. A quiet boy whom I at first thought to dislike me, I now know is simply shy. I have discovered he is a talented storyteller and his older brothers tease him unmercifully; as brothers are wont to do. I think I must speak with Niall about this son's future. He has the makings of a truly great Bard.*

*How can I think such things when I know what I must do? It seems an impossible task, to find Cathub, somehow obtain the crystal from around his neck, free my friends from his clutches and return us to our own time.*

## *Eighteen*

*Conochar, High King of Eire*

"My lord Conochar, it is a delightful surprise to find you at the head of such a fine army of warriors." Cathub bowed low before Conochar, the High King of the Ulaid.

"Your arrival is most timely. I will have your warriors made comfortable, and of course, you must have the best accommodations available. I will have this stone hut made ready for you immediately, my lord." It rankled Cathub so to have to bow and scrape before a man such as this. He, Cathub, who was the greatest Druid these people would ever know.

"I have provided for my own comfort, thank you, Cathub. My men will have my tents erected before you could have your own possessions removed from this hovel you presently inhabit."

"As you have undoubtedly been told, this upstart barbarian chieftain, Niall of the Eman Macha, has stolen your bride. I am told he plans to force her into marriage, my lord. Somehow they had been made aware of the time and place we would arrive, and lay in wait for us. They attacked your men just as we arrived from the Other World, where I had been keeping her safe for you."

Cathub studied the face of his king. The king had been a strapping, well-formed man of forty years when Cathub had first made his acquaintance. That would make him a mere fifty-five years of age now, although Conochar had not aged well since last Cathub visited, now five years past, to report on the welfare of the king's bride-to-be... and to collect the additional gold necessary for her upkeep, as well as the fine jewelry intended as gifts for the girl. All this, and more, was now safely tucked away in a safe located in Professor Walter Daniels' lab back in Dublin, in the year twenty-one hundred and six.

Cathub was not pleased to see the old king. His presence here could spell disaster. Conochar would insist on taking control of the siege. He may have aged badly, but Conochar was still a powerful warrior, as well as a brilliant strategist. He would eventually want to speak with Deirdre to ensure that she was still safe, and would find out that Cathub had misled them all.

He had known all along it was inevitable Conochar would eventually find out about his little deception. However, Cathub had intended that moment would not come until Deirdre had been married and he had collect his final reward from Conochar. He would then have returned to his own time, taking with him a treasure of gold, silver and jewelry, worth more than a king's ransom in the future.

"My King, my lord Cathub,"

*Would this Fedlimid be forever interrupting my contemplations*, Cathub thought.

Fedlimid continued, “One of the prisoners has escaped.”

“How is this possible, Cathub? Are you not the greatest Druid of our time? Are you not always telling me this? Who is it has escaped, Fedlimid?” Conochar’s continued jibes pricked at Cathub, but he would not allow anything to unsettle his supreme confidence.

“I have only just arrived, Cathub, and already there are problems. Deal with this at once.”

# *Nineteen*

## *Reunited*

"Deirdre, several of our warriors approach. I believe they bring good news. My father wishes you to accompany him. We are to meet him at the stables where the horses are being made ready." Ardan brought her this news.

A horse had not been prepared for Deirdre, as Niall already knew she did not possess the skill to ride alone. It also afforded her the opportunity to sit close and snuggle up against him.

*I don't know how much longer this man will be mine, but I am determined to enjoy every minute,* she thought. Excitement and dread commingled and colored her thoughts.

"What is this good news you speak of, Niall? Is it the crystal that Cathub wears around his neck? Have your men obtained it?" She prayed fervently that he would say yes, yet dreaded the same answer. It would mean Deirdre had no excuse to remain here; she would be able to return to her own time.

"No, *Cailín*, the Druid stays close to Conochar's warriors. He is protected at all times. I suspect he is aware that he is now the hunted. It is—" Just then the returning party came into view. Deirdre knew immediately what Niall's good news was for she immediately spotted Moira seated in front of one of the warriors. A particularly strapping man, a graybeard, as she had heard others refer to the older warriors.

"Moira!" Deirdre could not contain her excitement. "You're safe! Niall, you've found her, how can I thank you enough." Throwing her arms around Niall's neck she kissed him hard and soundly, nearly unseating them both.

"To see your pleasure at being reunited with your good friend is enough." Whispering into her ear, he continued, "Although your kisses are always welcome, perhaps in a more intimate surrounding, or at least a less precarious one." Laughing, Niall helped Deirdre from Bal's back so that she and Moira might embrace.

"I have missed you so much, Moira." Throwing her arms about her friend's neck, Deirdre hugged Moira to her. But her friend was more solemn.

"You must know that you are not safe. Walter Daniels has set himself up as a Druid priest called Cathub and he has—"

"We know, Moira. We know all of it. Niall's men have been following Cathub and Fedlimid from the beginning. I heard him speak of selling me into marriage with my own ears."

Deirdre's joy at being reunited with her friend was rapidly turning into sorrow as she brought Moira up to date. Fists clenched, Deirdre went on. "He will pay for the harm he has done. When Niall told me that you, Seamus and Charles had been made prisoners, when I heard him tell of how he would give me to this Conochar, I just wanted to throttle him." Shaking her fist, Deirdre looked as though she might actually take on the old Druid single-handed, causing Moira to grin for the first time in days. Deirdre, too, realized the humor of her declaration. Her anger left her as quickly as it had come and she smiled back at her friend.

"So, Deirdre, tell me, who are these men to whom I owe my rescue."

"Oh, I'm so sorry, I've forgotten my manners. Moira, this is Niall. He has saved my life more than once, and these are his sons, Naoisi and Ardan. They are responsible for every bit of information we have gathered about Cathub and his machinations. The graybeard I do not know, but it appeared to me that he had already introduced himself. This one is Ciran, and with him is his son, Arguile."

"Deirdre," Niall said, "I do not like to interrupt this reunion, however, we must return to the village. Cathub has sent to Conochar for more men. They are arriving at his camp even now. It will not be long before they are headed to the village."

"What of the people who do not live in the village? They will be in danger. We must warn them."

"The people have been warned. Even now they are arriving at the compound. You will have much company in the Great Hall."

The small company remounted their horses and made their way back to Niall's village. Deirdre now noticed what she had not noticed earlier; small groups of people with bundles upon their backs and loaded into small carts, making their way toward the village.

"How many men has Conochar sent? Niall, I cannot allow your people to suffer on my account. And what about Seamus and Charles? We cannot leave them at Cathub's mercy."

"My people are your people. They would never allow you to be taken against your will. Conochar has sent many men. You are a prize no man would want to lose, and Conochar has no love of being beaten. He is arrogant and foolish and the Eman Macha will best him. I intend that he should learn that lesson well."

"And you needn't worry about Charles and Seamus." Moira put in her two cents, "Cathub has won them over to his side with promises of wealth and power. As I understand it, they are to be his Druid assistants. I'm sorry, sweetheart, but it looks as though Niall and his people are our only hope."

"A siege." despair overtook Deirdre as she saw the number of people that had gathered inside the compound. "Niall, how long can your fortifications hold up against a siege? This is impossible. There are children here, how can they be protected? I cannot allow this. I will give myself up to Cathub. Perhaps I can persuade him to stop. I will appeal to his better nature."

"No! You will not go to that man. You are to be *my* wife. We have made promises to each other. And my promise to you was that I would protect you always, as I will in this. You will think no more to giving yourself over to Cathub."

"Wife! Deirdre is this true? Have you promised to marry Niall?" Moira's concern was very evident. In a quieter voice, she exclaimed, "Have you lost your mind, girl? You cannot do this!"

"Don't worry, Moira. I know what I must do when the time comes."

The sadness on Deirdre's face did little to ease Moira's apprehension. There was a very deep connection that had formed between these two. Moira could see how deeply Deirdre cared for Niall, and it was just as obvious that Niall loved Deirdre equally. Who would be more hurt by their departure when, and if, she and Deirdre ever recovered the time-travel devise that Cathub carried about his neck and were able to return to their own time?

# *Twenty*

## *Island Sanctuary*

The group relinquished their horses to a young boy who would take them to the stables to be fed and rubbed down, and headed towards Niall's stone rath, located very near the Great Hall. The warrior who Deirdre had come to think of as Graybeard had taken it upon himself to play host to Deirdre's friend. Deirdre grinned, it appeared Moira had also made a conquest.

"Niall." A thought began to formulate in Deirdre's mind, "The largest island we passed as we made our way to the burial island, it appeared to be uninhabited."

Confused by Deirdre's seemingly unrelated comment, Niall nevertheless responded, "It is not inhabited. There are no easy ways to approach this island, as vast boggy areas surround it, lying just below the surface of the water, which would swallow even our small craft whole, occupants and all. There is only one place where you can safely land a craft, and it takes great skill to approach even this relatively safe spot."

"But that would be perfect. We could move all of our people there. We would need tents, temporary shelters, plenty of food and fresh water. Are there enough skilled boatmen to move our people to the island safely, Niall? It doesn't matter." She waved the thought away. "The most skilled boatmen could navigate the way onto the island, marking the way as they go. The markers would serve to guide others along the safe route onto the island. Once everyone is on the island, the markers would be removed. Conochar's men do not have boats and even if they do, if they try to approach the island, they will not know where the safe route lies. Why do you grin at me so? Have I said something to amuse you?"

"No, *Cailín*, I do not laugh at you. You do not realize that you have just referred to the Eman Macha people as your own for the first time. You have accepted my people as your own."

"Well, of course I have." She touched his face tenderly. "You and the Eman Macha have been very good to me. You put yourself in danger for me, how can I not feel part of you? That is why I feel I must do everything I can think of to keep them safe."

"Aye, and is it only gratitude that brings these feelings?"

Resting her head against his chest, Deirdre sighed deeply. It was not possible to lie to him. "No, it is not only gratitude I feel for you, Niall. You know this. How could you not know how I feel for you after the nights we have spent together." Rearing back so she could look him straight in the eye, she continued, "but these people of yours... ours, are in danger, and I know this island is the answer to keeping them safe."

Deirdre's enthusiasm was infectious and Niall soon began to see the merit in her plan. The island would be a perfect place for his people to wait out the siege. It could be protected with a minimum of warriors, while the bulk of their forces held the compound against Conochar's invading forces.

"It could be done. Aye, it is a good plan, Deirdre. We can move the people in relative secrecy through the escape tunnel in the souterrain. I will have Ciran and Naoisi organize the move. It will have to begin immediately, as Conochar's men must surely be on their way."

Three hours later, reports came in that Conochar had indeed joined his army of warriors and was now in the enemy encampment preparing to march upon the village. Most of the people of the Eman Macha had been moved to the island with food and supplies for several weeks. The sheep and cattle were moved as well. Deirdre had no idea cattle could swim, but most of the cows and all the horses brought into the compound had been herded across the water to the island where they were now grazing contentedly on the tall lush grasses. The sheep were carried across in the little *curragh*, two or three at a time, each animal held tightly in the arms of a villager, for sheep could not swim and would sink like a rock should they fall into the water. Hide shelters could be seen going up all over the island as the men went about the task of ensuring their families were taken care of before heading back to the village compound.

Niall insisted Deirdre join the people in their temporary exile on the island and had found out just how independent his wife-to-be could be. She had rejected his order out of hand.

"I will not leave. Cathub must be confronted with what he has done, and I will be the one to do it. I will not allow that man to control my life any longer than he has already done. If I allow his presence to send me running for cover one more time, I am giving that control over to him without a fight."

"Deirdre, I can not do what must be done if I am not assured of your safety... you *will* go with the rest to the island, and you will go now." Certain of his ability to command, Niall was unprepared for Deirdre's adamant retort.

"No! No, I will not. The only way you will get me to turn and run from Cathub again would be to take me from here kicking and screaming. Not exactly the silent retreat you would prefer, I assume." Crossed arms and the defiant turn of her head told him Deirdre was not to be persuaded.

What Niall did next shocked Deirdre into silence. He picked her up as he had done so many days before, heaved her across his shoulder and headed across the nearly deserted compound toward the once crowded, now empty, Great Hall. Niall had called her bluff. She had never intended to scream and cause a scene. She would not call any unnecessary attention from the invading force on their way to their gates. Niall had known this.

Once inside the hall however, he did not head for the ladder leading into the souterrain, but rather to the ladder leading up to Deirdre's sleeping quarters.

Setting her back on her feet at the foot of the fur heaped pallet, Niall pulled his leather tunic over his head and tossed it aside.

"You are a defiant woman. I am your chieftain and soon will be your husband, and yet you defy me openly," Grinning at her lasciviously he spoke with a husky tone, "And I find that it excites me greatly." His face took on a look of mock speculation. "Perhaps I need to educate my wife-to-be in the proper way to *respond* to her husband."

Deirdre pulled the bindings from her hair and shook loose the long flaming-red tresses. "It is true, my chieftain, I think that my education has definitely been neglected of late and I am sadly ignorant of the ways of a wife here in your country." Loosing the ties of her own tunic, Deirdre soon had it off. The loose fitting woolen gown beneath soon followed her tunic to the floor.

Grabbing the waist of Niall's braecs, Deirdre pulled him to her. Running her hands possessively over the chiseled muscles of his bare chest and down over his hardened belly, Deirdre reveled in the taut muscular body of her man.

Undoing the leather girdle, which bound Niall's braecs, Deirdre's hands glided across inflexible skin, slipped beneath the waist of his breeches and held Niall's complete attention, even as he pulled her to him. With one hand he held her tightly against him, with the other he groped blindly for the pallet, guiding them both onto the fur coverings as her manipulative, massaging fingers elicited groans from deep within his throat.

His mouth and tongue sought and found that favored spot at the base of her throat where he felt the thrumming rhythm of racing blood as it pumped from her wildly beating heart. He lingered there, absorbing the rhythm, conscious of the extreme vulnerability of the woman who lay beneath him, giving herself up to him. Reluctantly leaving that warm sweet-tasting hollow, Niall's hot, seeking mouth trailed wet kisses down between taut, peaking breasts. Her back arched, her breasts already swollen with passion, Deirdre's nipples hardened and extended as Niall took each in turn into his mouth, suckling, laving each with the tip of his tongue. Deirdre tangled her hands in his long, russet hair, trying desperately to guide his face, that seeking mouth, down to the hot wet point where she spread herself for him.

But he would not be guided. Special attention, loving, tender, teasing attention must be given to each breast... each nipple, bringing her slowly, agonizingly to the point of desperation. Frantic, mindless thrusting of her pelvis brought a mischievous grin back to Niall's face. With agonizing slowness, he began to nibble gently at the soft, yielding flesh of Deirdre's belly, leaving a wet tongue-trail around, then dipping seductively into her bellybutton. As Niall teased the crisply curled, flaming red hair down between her legs with the flicking tip of his tongue, Deirdre's breathing came in harsh, panting gasps.

"Niall," she managed to whisper between shuddering gasps, "if you mean this as punishment, if this is the way you intend to discipline me for defying you, I guarantee I shall defy you at every opportunity."

Holding Deirdre's wildly bucking body and thrashing legs firmly in his arms, Niall buried his face in the warm, wet depths between her legs. Thrusting urgently against that hungry, seeking mouth, Deirdre's passion spent itself again and again, finally allowing her to collapse against the furs beneath her. But Niall had not yet finished with schooling his wife-to-be.

Flipping her exhausted body onto her stomach and kneeling on strong, heavily muscled legs, Niall caressed her silken inner thighs. Touching and exploring, he leaned down to kiss the sweetly dimpled inner knees. He moved his hands up to massage the muscles of Deirdre's buttocks, then encircled the tiny waist above those two luscious globes, Niall moved his hands upward to roam over Deirdre's narrow waist and back. He reveled in the taut, pliant flesh, the silken skin. Using his hands he explored beneath the trembling body lying beneath his. He felt the butterfly flutter of her belly muscles, as her passion again built beneath his caress. His hands roamed upwards again, to cup those breasts he had earlier so lovingly attended. Moving her great mass of hair aside, Niall kissed and nuzzled at her neck, then his tongue sought the ridge of her spine, pausing here and there to nibble at the pliant flesh, making his way slowly down the bony ridge. Deirdre moved beneath him, responding to his touch. Her breath again became ragged. She undulated against him, arousing his body with the sensual movement of her own.

Unable to control his own passion any longer, Niall turned Deirdre onto her back and her arms and legs wrapped about him, pulling him down and into her warm, consuming embrace. His mouth sought hers as he abandoned himself to the mindless culmination of both their passions.

Exhausted, Niall wanted nothing more than to collapse next to Deirdre and fold her into his arms so they might both drift off to sleep; however, their current plight would not allow such luxury. Niall fought off the desire to succumb to passion drugged sleep. The siege would begin soon, very soon, and Niall must be there with his men when it began.

It had been many years since he had felt such contentment. The warmth of a wife curled against his chest and he watched her as she fell into contented sleep.

It was that point in the season when night came earlier and earlier. He would have found himself in complete darkness had not some thoughtful fellow fed the fire in the hearth below, providing both warmth against the gathering cold of night, and a soft ambient light. Propping himself against the stony wall at his back, Niall pulled back the fur covering so that he might better see the woman sprawled over the full length of him. Again he felt the fragile vulnerability of this woman who had so firmly entangled herself around his heart. Barely controlled fear and a blinding fury threatened to boil up and choke him as he thought of the man out there somewhere who would take her from him and sell her to another for power and wealth.

Niall disentangled himself from Deirdre. After quickly pulling on his clothes, Niall woke her gently.

"It is time, *Cailín.* Dress quickly. I go now to arrange for one more *curragh* to go out to the island tonight. Like it or not, you will be safely out of Conochar's reach before the light of dawn."

Raising his hand to forestall any argument, Niall continued, "Do not argue. This is how it must be." He turned and went out into the clear, cool night. He needed to hear news of the enemy and to make final arrangements for the siege to come.

# *Twenty-one*

## *Siege*

As he walked the ramparts of the wall that protected his village, Niall's heart turned to lead in his chest. Conochar's warriors numbered two hundred easily and they ringed the fortified wall of the village. No attempt had been made to conceal them. Fires had been lit; Niall could taste the ash of their fires on the night air.

It is well they had removed the women and children hours before, as there was little hope of escape through the souterrain now. Deirdre would get her wish. She would not be forced to leave the village tonight for the danger of trying to move past the sentries outside the wall was greater than her remaining here with him. At least they were not greatly outnumbered. As in all things, Conochar had underestimated his enemy, believing himself to be all-powerful; he had failed to realize that Niall commanded well over one hundred warriors himself. Another five and twenty protected the island refuge. A prearranged signal fire would bring them to shore well behind the enemy lines where they might attack Conochar's warriors from behind. It was a drastic plan. One to be implemented only under the most dire circumstances.

Feeling Deirdre's presence beside him, Niall spoke softly, "Your wish has been granted, *Cailín*, you will not be sent away to the island tonight. Conochar's men have arrived, and the village is surrounded. We are under siege."

"Will he attack right away? What if he finds the entrance to the souterrain?" Deirdre spoke just as quietly.

"No, I do not believe he will attack right away. He will want us to look upon his great army. He believes us to be weak and does not know that our forces nearly equal his own. Also, he will not risk your being harmed in a pitched battle. As for the souterrain, men have been sent to ensure the entrance is well hidden. Heavy oak doors will be bolted shut and the men will stay to protect that entrance." Folding her into the warmth of his embrace, Niall felt Deirdre trembling against him.

"You are cold. You should move back to the warmth of the Great Hall. You should not be out here on the wall where anyone might see you. You are vulnerable up here."

"I'm not cold, Niall, I'm frightened. Frightened that I might lose you. You could be killed fighting for me. I feel sick to think that you... any one of these men, could lose your life because of me. We should all go to the island. If they burn the village, it doesn't matter. The village can be rebuilt."

"It is too late, Deirdre. It is too dangerous to move you, one small woman, past the line that has been drawn around this village. How would I move over one hundred men?"

"I have seen your men move silently through the forest. They move like an unseen breeze. They could go one by one. They would not be seen and they would be safe."

Niall could see that Deirdre was working herself into a panic.

"Calm yourself. My men are seasoned warriors. Conochar's men are soft, they are too used to men throwing down their arms before them. Look how they ran before the Eman Macha at the meadow just a few days previous. They steal cattle; they are not warriors. Now, will you go back to the Great Hall?"

"I feel safer here by your side, Niall. Please don't send me away yet. I could fight, you know. Don't laugh, I could!"

Niall nuzzled Deirdre's neck, inhaling the scent of her hair, which he knew would have the power to bring him to full arousal well into his dotage.

"Please, *Cailín*, take yourself back to the Great Hall. My mind must be on the matter at hand, not what you conceal beneath this thin gown."

Pouting, but at least temporarily obedient, she had agreed to remove herself from the immediate danger of the wall. Niall watched Deirdre make her way down the stone steps cut into the wall before turning his attention back to the matter at hand.

Niall called out to the invading force beyond the walls. "Druid, do you attend? What of you, Conochar, who calls himself King of all the One Hundred Tribes, do you speak with Niall of the Eman Macha? Or do you hide yourself behind your warriors? Where is this great Druid Cathub who would sell a woman into bondage for his own gain?" Niall was not sure whether or not deliberate provocation was a good idea, but it would end the waiting. In addition, if there were to be open battle, it would be to their advantage for Niall to choose the time when it came about.

"Send out the woman, Deirdre, unharmed and I will withdraw Lord Conochar's forces from your lands."

"It is not Cathub who speaks, nor is it Conochar. Is that Fedlimid? As I thought, old men too timid to face the treachery they have wrought."

"Aye, Niall, it is Fedlimid who speaks. Lord Cathub has agreed to forget that you have taken his foster daughter by force and will forgive your offense should you return the girl unharmed."

"By force? Sweet Brigit! She has run from the old conniver and sought sanctuary with my people. Deirdre has given her promise to me, not to that withered old man who set himself up as king. The Eman Macha will protect Deirdre, who is to be *my* wife, to the death, from the one who would sell her like a brooding cow for no more reason than to fatten his own purse. Have you all forgotten the laws of our people? No woman can be forced into marriage. And where is this King of yours who would buy a woman for his wife? Is he so old and ugly he can get no woman who is willing, but must take one against her will?"

*Well* he thought, *If that doesn't bring one or the other of the old goats out of hiding, nothing will.*

Outlined by the red glow of a fire, Niall saw the figure of Fedlimid clearly. A well-placed lance would effectively remove the head of this serpent. The night was a dark one due to a heavy cloud cover, and the moon had yet to rise. Fedlimid could not see Niall, he was sure of it. He would not see the lance coming until it was too late. It was not Fedlimid that threatened Deirdre's safety, but Cathub and Conochar. Killing Fedlimid would throw the invading force into chaos, but only temporarily. It would stop neither the Druid nor the King of the Ulaid.

Minutes passed. No one stepped forward, but a voice did ring out from the shadows behind Fedlimid.

"Why should I allow Deirdre, who is as dear to me as any daughter, to be wed to some barbarian who is no more than Chieftain of rabble, when she can be a queen? Conochar offers a throne to my Deirdre. What do you offer, Niall of Commoners? You say Deirdre has agreed to wed with you. How do I know this? I say you have ravaged my girl and forced her to this end, and will not believe she has agreed to this until I hear it from her own lips. Bring Deirdre forth that I might speak with her."

"Agreed, old man. Deirdre will stand here by my side and—"

"No! How do I know you will not hold a dagger to her back? Force her to speak your words? She must stand here before me and say that she prefers you."

"Do you think I would trust you, old man? You have already proven yourself unworthy of that trust. And what of Moira? Do you deny you held this woman prisoner because you believed she would warn Deirdre of your plot? Moira also will come forward and confirm that Deirdre has agreed to this marriage."

"And I have two who will witness that the woman Moira is a jealous harpy who is envious of the match I have made for Deirdre. It is she who is responsible for my Deirdre falling into your clutches. Only with her standing here before me, will I believe Deirdre rejects the match I have made for her."

"I will not allow her to venture outside these walls."

"I will accept no other terms."

"Then there is little else for us to speak of, Druid. Tell your master Niall of the Eman Macha will not bow to him, nor will I give up my woman to him."

To defy a Druid was not easily done. A Druid could call down the wrath of the gods upon them. Niall saw unease grow in his men. But the Eman Macha had Druids of their own. Niall had gone to them long before the siege had come upon the village and explained to them how the Druid Cathub had betrayed the trust of his foster daughter, all for his own gain. The Druids of the Eman Macha, men of his own clan, moved now through the ranks, reassuring his warriors, bolstering their courage.

Time would move slowly now. Fedlimid was an old campaigner, he would allow the tension to grow, hoping Niall's men would become restive and begin to question Niall's right to place their lives in danger for a woman who was not of their clan. He did not know that Deirdre had become one of them, had endeared herself to the people of the Eman Macha. Fedlimid did not know the weaker members of the clan, those who could not fight, had been removed from danger. He would believe the warriors would fear for the lives of their women and children, for their old ones. Aye, it would be some time before Fedlimid would move against them, thinking he held the advantage.

Niall, too, moved among the men who protected the wall, giving them encouragement, alleviating their fears. There were some women among the men. It was not unusual for young, strong women to fight along side their men. It was their right. Perhaps he should not have denied Deirdre the right to fight beside him. It was hard to know what was right.

He saw her standing in the entrance to the Great Hall, the little dirk he had given to her clutched in one hand. A great fire burned in the hearth within the hall, lighting the doorway, and Deirdre. Did he have the right to deny Deirdre the same right the other women of the clan have the benefit of; the right to fight for herself and her clan?

*She makes a brave figure standing with dirk in hand. Lighted from behind, she looks like the mother goddess Macha; patron goddess of the Eman Macha, ready to fight to protect her children.* Although what Niall wanted most was to protect her—was keeping her confined to the hall really best? For her and for their people? To see her like this, skirts kilted in her girdle, ready to fight with her people, to fight for the right to be one of the Clan Eman Macha—this would inspire the warriors to fight for her.

It would also show the men of the Ulaid that Deirdre had not been forced to join with Niall and his clan.

The whisper of *Macha* could be heard here and there upon the wall. It was not just he who saw the goddess image in Deirdre as she stood backlit in the doorway of the Great Hall, dirk in hand.

# *Twenty-two*

*The babe Deirdre*

"That unwashed, arrogant, ruffian. He thinks he dare defy Cathub? He thinks he dare defy you, My Lord Conochar?" Cathub's agitation drove him to pace. His distress was not due to Niall's defiance, no, he was not angry that Niall had refused to allow Deirdre to speak face-to-face with him. He had expected and wanted Niall to refuse. That was why he issued the ultimatum. By his refusal, Niall cast suspicion upon himself and away from Cathub. No, what Cathub feared most was that Conochar would intuit his purpose at issuing such a demand. He was afraid of Conochar and what he would do should he find out about his machinations, about his deceptions, about his betrayal.

Of course, he could always use the crystal to return to his own time, and begin again. No, no he would not give in to this rabble. He'd spent years working on this plan; he would not abandon it now.

When he had first journeyed back to this era and met Conochar, he had ingratiated himself to the great King of the Ulaid. Cathub spent several months in the company of the king, hoping to someday profit from the acquaintance. Little did he realize that upon his second visit to the Celtic king, his efforts would already reap him a well-deserved reward.

When the wife of Fedlimid had begged him to forecast her unborn child's future, the child had indeed spoken to him, but not in the form of prophecy. A plan had come to him, full blown, a plan to make him the most powerful figure of this age. He convinced Conochar that the child about to be born to Fedlimid would grow up to be his wife; a woman of great beauty, who would bring him great fame. He also convinced Conochar that the child should be raised away from the society of Ulaid warriors, to keep her pure for him. Cathub had even named the child Deirdre, after his own mother.

Conochar had practically thrown gold and silver at him for the child's upbringing so he had taken the child and the loot and had returned to his own time. Collectors were willing to pay millions for the ancient artifacts, especially artifacts in such fine undamaged condition.

It had been a simple matter to find a couple willing to raise the girl as their own, in return for financial support for their research.

Cathub, or rather Professor Daniels, had been mildly amused and somewhat flattered when he had come across an ancient Irish myth; Deirdre of the Sorrows. The tale spoke of a female child called Deirdre, a great Druid seer called Cathub, and the Ulaid king, Conochar. There had been a lot of nonsense about betrayal and death, but the gist of the myth was true—the portend of the child who would become the bride of Conochar.

Deirdre was not aware of it, but she was that child. She was Deirdre of the Sorrows, and it was her fate to be wed to Conochar. Cathub had taken her as a newborn babe from the hands of the mid-wife and transported her directly to his own time; then the year twenty eighty-two. He had waited twenty-four years for this moment, although only sixteen years had passed for Conochar.

Now, Cathub had to prevent Conochar from discovering Deirdre's willing part in this disastrous alliance with Niall. The disaster would be to Cathub, of course. *What else mattered?*

"There you have it, my lord. It is proven, as I told you, Niall of the Eman Macha has taken Deirdre by force. If she were a willing participant in this marriage, he would allow the girl to speak to me directly. Without a dagger at her back, she would not willingly marry this barbarian and he knows it."

"I heard what was said Cathub. It would seem Niall of the Eman Macha fears for the girl's safety. He speaks of treachery. What treachery is this? Is this some unfortunate girl you have taken from her family against her will, or is this the daughter of Fedlimid I gave into your care six and ten years previous to be raised as my future wife?" Before Cathub could declare his innocence, Conochar raised a warning hand.

"Think carefully before answering, Druid. Remember, I placed my mark upon that child. The image of my ring was branded into the heel of the child, which will tell me immediately if this be the one and only Deirdre, daughter of Fedlimid."

"The brand is there, my lord. There is no doubt."

"Is it true, my lord? This woman, this child, Deirdre, is my own babe? I was told my child had died. You allowed me to believe all these years my child had died. Knowing my wife had broken her body and her spirit trying to have another child, you allowed us to believe this child was lost to us?"

"Aye, Fedlimid, I do you the honor of taking your only daughter as my wife." Neither Conochar nor Cathub noticed the stricken face of Fedlimid and his shaking hand, as he drew back the tent flap and stumbled, unnoticed into the night.

"Cathub, let us retrieve what is mine, then raze this village to the ground."

Chanting and the sounds of weapons clashing brought both King and Druid out of the tent and to the line of warriors that ringed the village walls.

# *Twenty-three*

*Macha*

As Deirdre moved from the Great Hall across the open compound towards the fortified wall, she heard the unmistakable sound of an iron sword being brought up sharply against a bronze shield, then again, and yet again; creating a steady rhythm that matched her footsteps. Another warrior took up the beat, then another, and another.

Dagger in hand, wild red tresses swirling about her head, she knew instinctively she must show herself, and stand beside these men who would gamble their lives to protect her. Her instincts also told her that she could become the galvanizing force that would bring these warriors together and defeat Conochar and his Ulaid invaders.

Reaching the top of the wall, Deirdre took up a shield, and herself began the steady beating of weapon against shield, and even over the noise of metal striking metal she heard the cry of *Macha, Macha, Macha*, grow. Moving to a place on the wall where she knew those who threatened the village walls from below would see her, Deirdre called out.

"You there who would take me against my will. I will stand beside Niall and the Eman Macha to defend these walls with my life. You will not have me, Conochar of the Ulaid, for I choose the Eman Macha!"

As she raised her dagger to the sky, a great roar went up from the defenders. The cry of *Macha, Macha, Macha* and the steady drumming of the shields grew deafening. Niall stood behind her, both arms raised, hands empty as if to show all that he did not force her to speak these words.

The warriors below drew back; an involuntary reaction to the wild-eyed woman standing upon the wall, dagger in hand, flaming red hair swirling about her head, and to the rising chant to the goddess *Macha.*

The chanting ceased as suddenly as it had begun, as if from a signal. Conochar stepped forward into the light of the fire, his form brightly illuminated. A cold sweat of dread broke out across her forehead, and a gripping knot of fear clenched at her stomach. Deirdre recognized the feeling of events spiraling out of her control.

"Niall, Chieftain of the Eman Macha. It becomes evident to me that the Druid Cathub has perpetrated a great injury upon us all. Come forward, sit with me, parlay, and all will be forgiven. Bring Deirdre with you that I may make reparation for the part I have unwittingly played in this unfortunate incident."

"Do you think I would trust you, Conochar? Conochar, who has sent men to raid Eman Macha cattle for these two seasons? Conochar, who even now lays siege on Eman Macha land?"

"I will send Fedlimid to you so that you may be assured my intentions are honorable."

And it was true. The tall, gray-haired warrior stepped from the shadows and moved toward the barred gates, empty hands held high. Deirdre watched from the wall as the men, at Niall's command, opened the gates, allowed Fedlimid to step through, then swiftly barred the gates again behind him. Convinced it was yet another deception, doubt gnawed at her. Deirdre moved swiftly to join Niall and together they advanced to where the Ulaid warrior stood at the gate.

"Niall, you must not trust Conochar."

"Hush, *Cailín*, I know, but I would hear what Fedlimid would say to me."

It was a strange sensation that overcame her as Deirdre came at last into the presence of Fedlimid, the man who had led an army into enemy lands to take her. It was not the fear or rage she would have expected. Looking into the eyes of the man who had figured prominently in her nightmares of the last several days, she saw pain. Pain and regret. And the anger would not come to her.

Deirdre's jaw dropped open as Fedlimid knelt on one knee before her, took her hand in his and pressed it to his lips.

"My daughter, my child. So long it has been that your mother and I felt the pain of your loss."

She tugged her hand from his grasp. "What is he saying, Niall? You can not be my father, sir." Addressing herself to Niall and Fedlimid alternately, Deirdre faltered, "Niall, tell this man he is not my father!"

"It is true, child. I heard it from Conochar and Cathub no more than moments past. Your mother and I were told you had died at birth, now I learn Conochar had you secreted away by this most foul Druid, raised you away from your parents who have grieved for your loss." To Niall he said, "We must speak, sir. Conochar has treachery in mind. We must act quickly to thwart him and we have only moments before he becomes suspicious."

"Do you expect me to believe you have suddenly changed sides, Fedlimid? That you now wish to help us?"

"It is understandable you would question my motives. I have served Conochar all of my life, for he is my king. But you must understand, I have just now learned that the man... the king I have always trusted and followed without question, had my only child stolen from me almost at the moment of her birth. I have only just now taken my first look at the face of my own daughter. This man has stolen my life from me. My wife was never again able to give birth to a living child. She died at an early age, stricken by grief, her body broken by her great need for a child. I will not have my only child given in marriage to such as him. Now, can we speak of what must be done?"

"Wait. Wait. I cannot be your child, Fedlimid. I was born very, very, far from here. It is not possible."

"It is easy to prove. I heard Conochar and Cathub speak of a brand burned into the heel of the infant... my infant girl, moments after her birth." He did not have to continue. Deirdre was sure the truth must be written all over her face. Even Niall knew the truth of Fedlimid's declaration. He had himself commented on the odd markings upon the heal of her foot.

"When I was very young," Deirdre spoke, mostly to herself, "I asked my father... my adopted father, how I had received the odd scar on my foot and he told me that as a baby, I had stepped on a very, very hot manhole cover, umm, I mean shield, and the hot metal had left this scar. Now that I hear myself say it out loud, I realize how unbelievable it sounds." She looked to Niall for direction.

Deirdre began to sway. Niall's face, full of concern, peered into hers, and faded just as her vision went black.

When she awoke, she was in Niall's arms and the three of them were just entering the Great Hall. He placed her gingerly upon her feet but kept a steadying hand hovering at her back.

"I have a father. I have a real father. All my life I felt as though I was an unwanted burden. When I became older, I couldn't help but wonder why my parents had adopted me since it was so obvious they neither wanted nor had any interest in me. Now I discover I was stolen from my real parents at birth, that I had parents who mourned my loss."

Looking at Fedlimid timidly, Deirdre ventured to ask, "If you are indeed my father, may I call you *Da* as I have heard Niall's own children call him?"

Crushing her in a bear hug, Fedlimid lifted Deirdre from her feet. He sniffled back tears as he said, "I have waited all my life to hear a child of mine speak those words. Of course you may call me *Da*! And when there is time, I shall speak to you of your mother."

Pushing her gently from him, the old warrior swiped at his eyes, and addressed himself to Niall.

"Niall of the Eman Macha, you will call forth witnesses to attend us."

Moving to the door of the hall, Niall called out to the Druid Pádraig, and his friend, Ciran, who loitered just outside.

When the men entered the room expectantly, Fedlimid continued. "Druid, remember this well. Niall, Chieftain of the people known as the Eman Macha, I, Fedlimid, sire of Deirdre, do give my daughter to you to be taken as your wife in marriage. As marriage price, my daughter will be provided with the following dower. The lands her mother brought with her as her dowry in her marriage to me, which do border upon Eman Mach lands to the north, as well as six plates of gold and twelve of silver. Also will she have her mother's bronze and amber necklaces and girdle, as well as gold and enamel rings, and the jeweled casket in which they reside. Do you accept Deirdre as your betrothed, and the dowry she brings?"

"I would accept her if she brought nothing more than the gown she wears. I welcome you who is to be father-in-law to me to the Clan of the Eman Macha. From this day we will call you kinsman."

"Very well. Druid, we will no doubt have need of your magic before this day is gone. Let us sit and discuss my plan. We must be swift. Conochar will grow restive and there is no time to waste." They all gathered about the old warrior at one of the tables where food had been laid out. It was but poor fair. A shoulder of pork and a leg of lamb, both cold, smoked salmon, bread and cheese. There were none to prepare hot food for the warriors, but provisions had been left so that they might keep up their strength during the siege to come.

# *Twenty-four*

*The Legend Ends...*

It was well into night before the gate to the beleaguered village opened again, allowing Fedlimid to step out from the stockade. Making his way slowly over the grass-covered grounds that lay between the fortified walls and the invading forces, his unprotected back providing an easy target, Fedlimid thought about what he must do. The life of his only child, as well as her future happiness, weighed in the balance. It pleased him to know that it was he who would be, in some small way, responsible for his daughter achieving that happiness.

Cathub reacted with a mad giggle at the broad grin that could be seen to stretch across the old warrior's face, as Fedlimid approached his liege lord and the Druid.

"It would appear our plan will be successful, my lord." The whisper of aged skin chafing against itself came to Fedlimid as the old man in the druid garb rubbed his hands in gleeful anticipation. His own skin crawled as he observed how Cathub could transform himself from arrogant condescension to obsequious servility with flawless ease.

"So it would seem, Druid. Fedlimid, tell me what has transpired." Conochar's behavior towards Cathub seemed to match Fedlimid's; growing distrust combined with rigorous distaste.

"My lords," making obeisance first to the King then, with obvious revulsion, to Cathub, Fedlimid proceeded. "Niall has agreed to come forward to speak with you, my lord. He was less inclined to agree to Deirdre accompanying him. He fears still for her safety."

"And yet he has agreed?" Conochar's eager query did much to quiet Fedlimid's unease. A man so fervent for a woman he had yet to see since a nursing babe, would willingly leap from the cliff's edge, once led to it, if the promise of the woman he desired lie at the cliff's foot. Most especially if that man believed the leap to be part of his own collusion.

"Yes, my lord. Niall has agreed, but only if you will give your promise of their safe conduct to Pádraig, who is Druid to the Eman Macha."

"Agreed." Again, the enthusiastic response for which Fedlimid had hoped.

"There is more, my lord. Soon, when the moon is high, Niall and Deirdre will exit the village through the gates just there, come to a point midway between the village walls and our camp. They will be accompanied by three of Niall's most trusted warriors. They will be armed, though Niall will come without weapons. Once the promise has been made before their Druid, I am to come forward and stand with Niall's men, as hostage, while Niall and Deirdre come the rest of the way to parlay."

"Again, agreed. This will fit our plan perfectly. You know what you must do, Fedlimid. You will wait for my command then strike."

Cathub kept his silence until that moment. Fedlimid watched the Druid closely as Conochar and he had gone over Niall's requirements. He would be trouble, there was no doubt. Fedlimid allowed his hand to rest lightly upon the hilt of his sword. Perhaps Cathub's madness had not so fuddled the man's brains, as Fedlimid had first believed.

"My lord. I do not like the sound of this plan. You place too much control in the hands of this rabble prince. You must not allow Niall to bring armed warriors with him. You cannot truly be considering leaving Fedlimid within Niall's power. I demand you give..." Conochar cut Cathub short and Fedlimid knew without doubt the Druid had made a fatal error.

"I *must. You* do not like my plan. You *demand.* You dare to tell Conochar what he must do, to question my decisions? Fedlimid, I weary of this old man. Put him under guard until I decide what is to be done with him."

The first waves of fear begin to penetrate Cathub's madness and began to take firm hold upon his mind. His hand moved to take hold of the time-travel crystal, which hung heavily about his neck. What Conochar did next threw him into panic.

"Wait, Fedlimid." Reaching toward Cathub, Conochar took hold of the crystal before Cathub could activate the device. Conochar began to lift the Druid's symbol of power from about Cathub's neck.

"Fedlimid, take this trinket as a gift to my lady, that she might know the generosity of Conochar. Tell her it is a peace offering. By giving her this gift, she will know her King, and future husband, intends to deal harshly with the traitorous Cathub."

Snatching the crystal from the startled king's hand, Cathub swirled and stepped back from the King.

"You dare to touch the crystal of the great Cathub? You think an insignificant mortal like you could imprison the greatest Druid ever known? I will show you power the like of which you have never seen. Behold the awesome power of Cathub!"

It was unfortunate Cathub was unable to demonstrate for the King that power, for Fedlimid's sword flashed, removing the old man's head from his shoulders and separating the old Druid from the crystal he valued so much, as it dropped from his headless neck. Retrieving the crystal, and wiping the blood from the heavy silver chain, Fedlimid addressed his king with a bow.

"I shall deliver your gift personally, my lord." Calling two of his men to him, Fedlimid gave instructions for the removal of the formerly great Cathub.

Looking toward the east, Fedlimid commented, "It is time, my lord, the moon is fully risen, though it be obscured by heavy cloud."

Even as he spoke, the gates of the village swung open. Five figures appeared and hesitated before moving across the neutral zone that lay between the two opposing forces. Mists had begun to creep and swirl about their feet.

"Even in this darkness, you must identify Deirdre beyond doubt, before striking. Do not allow this Niall to substitute another for my Deirdre. Do you understand, Fedlimid?"

"Aye, my lord. Have no doubt, I will ensure that all is as it should be before proceeding." Fedlimid took care that the hatred he now felt for his king did not show on his face.

The heavy cloud cover roiled above, scudding across the darkened sky, moving the party in and out of dark moon-shadow.

The wall of the village was lined with armed warriors, intent upon two lone figures that walked ahead, followed closely by three with swords drawn. The small group stopped halfway between the warring camps.

The warriors lining the wall parted to reveal a solitary figure directly above the still open gates. As the figure raised his arms to the heavens, the concealing clouds pulled back as if upon command, allowing the light of the moon to fall full upon the Druid Pádraig.

"Conochar of the Ulaid. It is time to come forward. I am Pádraig, Druid of the Eman Macha, and I charge you to come forward."

"What is this, Fedlimid? I thought the Druid would come to me to exact this promise? Why does he stand there upon the wall and call to me? Am I to stand here and shout back and forth with this Druid before this entire company?"

"I do not know, my lord. We spoke of a promise to be given, the means of delivering that promise was not discussed."

"Well, there is nothing to do but proceed."

Calling out, Conochar answered Pádraig. "I am here, Druid. What is it you ask of me?" Conochar had advanced to the fore of his waiting warriors.

"Only this, Conochar. Before our Lady of the Moon, She who sees all from Her throne there in the night sky, and before these men gathered here, you must give promise of safe conduct to Niall of the Eman Macha and the Lady Deirdre, that they may enter your camp, give parlay, and return safely to these walls. Before all, do you swear? Say it!"

"Aye, I do give my promise."

"Speak the words, Conochar."

"I, Conochar, High King of the Ulaid, do before this assembly of men, give promise of safe conduct to Niall and Deirdre, that they may safely enter this camp, and return in safety to the Eman Macha village. They shall not be molested, nor shall harm come to them by my hand or that of any other within my command. This I do so swear."

"Very well, Conochar. Should you prove false... should any harm befall either, at your hand or be it caused by your word, The Lady of the Moon, She who is Mother to us all, will make your treachery known to all. Her back shall be turned to you and all the Ulaid."

Intent upon the small group who awaited his approach, Fedlimid moved forward.

"Daughter." Bowing before Deirdre, Fedlimid brought out the crystal intended as a gift from Conochar. Fedlimid had not believed his luck when Conochar had instructed him to give the necklace to Deirdre, knowing full well from their earlier meeting that Deirdre prized this bauble above all else.

"Conochar wishes you to accept this gift as a token of his ardor. And *I* intend it as a wedding gift to my daughter." As Fedlimid lifted the freshly polished chain to place it about his daughter's neck, Deirdre dropped the hood of the heavy mantle she had worn against the cold of the night. The moon, now fully risen, shone down upon her flaming red hair leaving little doubt to those watching that this was indeed the same woman who had railed against Conochar from the village wall.

"Let us proceed then." Upon cue, Niall and Deirdre linked hands and walked towards the waiting enemy. Stepping swiftly from behind, Fedlimid drew his sword, raised it high and struck Niall down, then drew swiftly down upon Niall's three bodyguards.

"Stand back, I do not wish to harm you."

Speaking loudly over Deirdre's mournful wails so as to be heard by the waiting witnesses on both sides, Fedlimid called out so all would hear. "It is by order of the High King, Conochar, Niall of the Eman Macha is struck down for the crime of taking that which belongs only to Conochar."

Just as swiftly, Deirdre snatched the dagger from Fedlimid's side, and called out, "Conochar, you would possess by deceit and betrayal that which is not yours to take. You shall never have me, nor shall any other but Niall. Even in death, I say to you, I choose Niall and the Eman Macha." Then, before those who watched in horror, knowing they were unable to prevent the tragedy, Deirdre plunged the blade into her breast and fell across Niall's bloody body.

Conochar's shrieks of "No, No, No," echoed across the eerily silent field as he charged across the grassy verge, roaring as if a wounded bull.

"By the Gods, Fedlimid, how could this happen?" Anguish colored the old King's words as they tore from his throat.

Pulled up short by the bloody scene before him, Conochar begged, "Turn her over, Fedlimid, let me look just once upon the face of my betrothed."

Fedlimid's dagger, still clutched in her hand, protruded from Deirdre's finely embroidered tunic, ruined now by the blood that soaked it. She still lived, and made feeble attempt to speak, although her voice did seem to carry well on the still, chilly night air.

"Father," she called out, "I would join my husband on his journey into the Other World. Do not allow this villain to possess me in death as he would have in life."

"Aye, daughter, it will be done."

Having spoken her desire to be laid to rest with Niall, Deirdre fell silent. Her breast no longer took in breath.

Signaling to Niall's men to remove the two fallen lovers, Fedlimid quickly turned Conochar aside.

"My lord. It is time to quit this place. My child will remain here with the man she has chosen as her husband."

Nodding his head in agreement, Conochar watched as the bodies of Deirdre and Niall were borne off into the silent walls of the Eman Macha.

Fedlimid led his King back to the waiting Ulaid warriors. A wave of whispered comments moved not so quietly through Conochar's men. Their king, long held to be a man of honor, had betrayed his word before them all. He had given safe conduct to the two ill-fated lovers and had, without a qualm, ordered the murder of one and caused the death of the other. If Conochar had forgotten the Druid's words, they had not... nor had Pádraig.

# *Twenty-five*

*Retribution*

Deirdre very nearly ruined the whole effect of her death scene by giggling into Ardan's shoulder as he carried her across the field and through the gate and into the compound.

"Quiet, woman," Ardan hissed between clenched teeth, "or we shall none of us live long enough to see you wed to my father. I would like to call you Mother at least once."

She could barely breathe due to the pig's bladder tightly strapped to her chest. Her gown was sticky with the blood of that same pig. If she didn't giggle, she felt she might scream.

As they entered the compound and the gates closed behind them, Ciran and Arguile dumped Niall to the ground without ceremony.

"Sweet Brigit, man! You weigh as much as a full grown bull," grumbled Ciran.

"Aye, well at least it was not my lifeless body you carried from the field."

"I thought the man had killed you for sure, Niall," Arguile spoke. "Even though I knew the plan, it looked so real as the blade struck. If you had not winked at me, I might well have put my blade into the man."

"Aye, well, it's done now isn't it, and no one has died." Slapping Arguile on the back, Niall called up to the Druid still standing on the fortified wall. "Are you ready then, Pádraig?"

"Aye, Niall, just a moment more," came his answer.

They all turned to watch the moon, now a bright silver disk directly above. Moments passed and Deirdre caught no change in the moon's appearance, but evidently Pádraig did, for his voice rose up and carried across to the Ulaid camp.

"Conochar, you have played false. You have betrayed your word before the Lady of the Moon and all these men assembled. Behold how The Lady repays your faithlessness." Holding his staff over his head, the Druid pointed to the moon.

The wind blew stronger, swirling the ground mists into a flurry, clouds scudded across the heavens, though none obscured the moon as She began slowly to remove Herself from the night sky.

A great subdued "Ahhhh," went up from the Ulaid warriors gathered below as, subtly at first, then more and more obviously, the great disk of the moon began to darken. Beginning in the lower quadrant and looking like great bites had been taken out of the very moon Herself, She began to disappear. It did look, thought Deirdre, as thought the moon was actually turning away.

"Behold, Conochar, The Lady turns her face from you and all the Ulaid who follow you."

Calls could now be heard from the Ulaid camp as men began to point up at the disappearing moon and shout to each other. Many could be seen to throw themselves upon the ground in fear, while others turned on the lone figure of the king even as they drew away from him. They were angry, frightened men, but none would come near the King who would now feel the wrath of the Goddess. Shouts of "dishonored," and "liar," carried across to those who watched with interest from the walls that so recently had been laid under siege. Conochar's warriors would follow him no more.

*At last Conochar will reap what he has sown*, thought Deirdre. *The days of running from him are past.*

"What must I do to redeem myself, priest?" Deirdre was surprised to see that Conochar had come forward.

"I am a broken man. I have lost the woman I have waited for these six and ten years to come join me as my wife. I confess freely that it is through my own machinations death has visited both sides of this wall."

"You are both right and wrong, Conochar. Your man has struck down Niall who was Chieftain of the Eman Macha, and it is because of your betrayal, Deirdre has been lost to the Eman Macha. My people will mourn the loss of Niall and Deirdre. The Bards will sing songs and recite great poems of what has passed here this night. What you have lost is your honor. You have lost the goodwill of the Goddess. Why should The Lady forgive your transgression?"

"Because I also have suffered. I have waited long years for my bride to come to me, only to have her choose death rather than be joined with me."

Niall joined the Druid at the top of the wall, taking care not to be seen by those who watched from the Ulaid camp. What was left of the moonlight shone upon the pig's blood, which covered his face, arms and shoulders. A similar pig bladder to the one Deirdre had had strapped to her chest, had been concealed within the folds of Niall's cloak and had burst upon being struck by Fedlimid's sword, spraying him with the swine's blood.

The Druid Pádraig once again called out to Conochar, "Our Lady of the Moon would know that the warriors of the Ulaid would follow Conochar no longer. What say you, warriors?"

To a man, backs were turned upon the old king, and the men of the Ulaid walked away.

"I would have him suffer longer, but the wheel it does turn," Pádraig whispered to Niall. Returning to his full voice, the Druid again addressed Conochar.

"Very well, Conochar. You who are king without warriors to follow you, the Lady takes pity upon you in your loss. She once again turns her face toward you. Leave the land of the Eman Macha now, and venture here no more." Staring once again at the near dark moon,

Deirdre could see that it was not a full eclipse and the moon was once again returning to her full brilliance.

Pádraig was indeed a master Druid. He had timed the lunar eclipse with the precision of a scientist from her own time who had the benefit of the most modern computers at his fingertips. Ah, but it was *not* her time, was it? *Best not to dwell upon it now*, she thought as she fingered the crystal hanging between her breasts.

# *Twenty-six*

*Moira*

"You will do what you must, Deirdre, but for myself I think I shall stay," for days Moira had thought hard about what she would say to Deirdre when this time came, as she knew it would.

"Paídín, the one you call graybeard, has asked that I become his wife. I like this place, and I can have a life here. But you must do what you think best for you."

"Stay! Moira, how can to say that? What is there here for us? This is not our time. Yes, I admit I was born here, but aside from the few hours spent here as an infant, this is a foreign land to us."

*The girl is talking herself out of the life that is meant for her here*, Moira thought. *She is young and does not know the value of finding that one person in the entire universe who is meant for you.*

"Moira, when you first heard of my betrothal to Niall, you chastised me for it. Told me I was crazy for agreeing."

"I did, and I was wrong. Do you really believe you will find a man in our time who will devote himself to you as Niall has done? What do you have there to return to... no friends, no money, and no family? Walter Daniels saw to it that you would have none there to look for you, no one who would miss you should you disappear. Look at what Niall and his people have done to protect you with only knowing you a few short days. Think on this, my girl... who back there is looking for you right now, and who here will search for you until the end of time should you disappear from this place?"

Moira left Deirdre with her thoughts. No amount of argument could force her to make the right choice; this was a decision she must make for herself, just as Moira had had to make her decision, by herself, without asking advice from Deirdre.

She would stay with Paídín, and who knows, she was only forty-one years old, perhaps she would have that child she had so desperately wanted all of her life. If not, Paídín had children and grandchildren enough to satisfy her. He had a stone rath with wattle fencing that stood practically in the shadow of the village walls. Several head of the clan cattle belonged to Paídín and he even had a plate or two of silver; making him a pretty good catch.

And he was a good man. He might be a little long in the tooth, although fifty-one would not be considered old in her time, Moira had to admit she would probably not have many years to enjoy Paídín's company. Perhaps with some modern day nutrition and health practices, Moira could extend that just a bit. Most importantly, he offered Moira a life she would not have had in her own time.

Those men who had been her colleagues would admire her mind, speak in glowing terms about her research and journal papers, but never did one of them look at her as a woman to be desired. Paídín had. The time they had spent exiled to the island; Moira as one of those to be protected, Paídín as one of those who protected them, the two had gotten to know each other well... very well.

He had asked her to belong to him, had promised to devote what was left of his life to her. There was a time when a declaration of that nature would have raised the ire of the feminist in her. Not now. She had thrown her arms around his neck and kissed him hard, right on the lips. Things had taken their own turn from there and they had spent little time out of each other's sight since then.

A sentry called out from the walls, disturbing her thoughts and announcing the approach of a lone rider. Moira ran to see who approached, as did everyone else in the compound.

It was Niall who greeted the visitor by pulling him from the horse's back and clasping him in a warm hug.

"Father-in-law, it is good to see you have survived Conochar's wrath. Have you come to join the Eman Macha?" Slapping his father-in-law good-naturedly on the back, Niall led him toward the Great Hall, where he would be treated as an honored guest. Perhaps, thought Moira, this is what would tip the balance and help Deirdre with the decision with which she wrestled.

"Nay, son. Conochar is a broken man. There are no teeth left in the great King of the Ulaid. Few warriors warm themselves at Conochar's fires these days. Those who do are of no account. I will wait a few months, retire to my new land, which I have just acquired from one who has for many years admired my lands on the coast. It was a good trade, as this new land just happens to border on Eman Macha land. By the time of the gathering of your clansmen in the spring, Fedlimid will be seen no more at Conochar's court. Perhaps by then you will have got my daughter with child and I can look forward to becoming an old man doting upon my grandchildren."

*Yes, give her something more to cling to in this world, old man.* But Moira saw nothing but pain and indecision etched in Deirdre's face as the group approached her there, where Moira had left her, outside the Great Hall.

"And what of the two called Seamus and Charles, Fedlimid?" Moira could not help but ask. Those two had been so easily turned by Cathub and his plot against Deirdre. Their early concern for her safety was so easily put aside by the promises of Celtic gold made by the mad old man who had fancied himself a great Druid priest, and had ended his life at the point of a sword.

"They have escaped. The confusion and turmoil of that night gave them the perfect opportunity to steal away. I do not think we need fear them, what harm can they do?"

"As long as they are out there, Deirdre is in danger. They will do anything to obtain the Druid's Crystal, even if it means doing harm to our Deirdre." Turning to Niall, Moira did her best to get them to understand the danger.

"Please, Niall, you must find these men. They are not equipped to survive in this world of yours without Cathub. They will be desperate. Find them, and kill them if you must."

## *Twenty-seven*

*Journal Entry*
*Deirdre*

*It has been three days since Niall and I played out our death scene for the benefit of the invading horde of Conochar's men. I have spent that time in continual turmoil, arguing with myself over what I must do next.*

*Moira has just left me. I had thought Moira would support my decision to return to the Twenty-second Century. Didn't she tell me not to become involved with Niall, not to give him my promise to marry him? Now she tells me not only should I stay, but also that she will not return with me should I decide to leave. One who I was sure I could count on has abandoned me.*

*My father, Fedlimid... how strange it is to say those two words and feel love in the saying of them... has come twice. Once for my "funeral" and again to say he will be leaving with Conochar. Before leaving, he asked Niall for safe passage that he might be there at the gathering of the Eman Macha clans next spring, to celebrate our marriage.*

*Now, suddenly, he has appeared at our gates once more. Every time I see him, I find I love him more and more... my father.*

*How can I bear to tell him that my marriage to Niall will not take place?*

*I have kept Niall away from me for these many days. It was not an easy thing to do. I have asked Levarcham, Niall's daughter, to stay with me in the Great Hall. I told Niall I needed to get to know the girl better, and that there are many plans which must take place before her betrothal this coming spring. I think he was very hurt by this, but I have to if I am to make the decision I know I must.*

*What I don't understand is why I haven't just left already. Moira, bless her heart, has said I must take my time and that I will know what is right, when the time is right. But I know she expects me to stay.*

*This is to be the final entry in this journal. It brings me nothing but pain to see it... to read what I put down on paper. When I close this entry, I will bury my journal here beneath the floor of the Great Hall. I never want to see it again!*

# *Twenty-eight*

## *Pain and Pleasure*

"Da, what do you do here alone?" It was Naoisi who found Niall down at the lakeshore, staring across to the little island where his people had hidden during Conochar's siege.

"This siege has given me much to think on. Our people need a permanent place of refuge during times of danger such as we just saw. This little island is a perfect place for just such a refuge. I will build a Great Hall there for Deirdre. She tells me the dwellings in her land have living spaces that stack one upon another, up into the sky. I will build her such a dwelling. There will be homes for each of my sons on this island, and dwellings to store food for our people so that when danger comes, we will be prepared to protect them. There is plenty of pasture for the cattle and sheep. We will do well there. I will cross now to the island to look for the best building sites."

"Da, your face no longer hides what you feel. Since Deirdre has come into our lives, everything you feel is written there upon your face for all to see. And your face right now tells me it is not building sites you think of. You are in pain. Something is wrong, Da, and I will ask you again, what do you do here alone?"

Niall thought, not for the first time in these past several days, that his son was no longer the boy he had been. He had become a good and caring man, intelligent and sensitive. He would make a good leader for their people. But Niall was not ready to speak of his thoughts to anyone, let alone his son. His thoughts and his pain were his own.

"What cause do you have to think there is aught wrong?"

"Besides the look of pain and hurt you wear on your face, besides Deirdre locking herself away in the Great Hall with none but her women to keep company with her, besides your removing yourself from the village as often as possible? No cause, no cause at all."

"I do not remove myself from the village. I am Chieftain of the Eman Macha and as such there is business I must attend. I have many things I think on, the sites for our new buildings is but one. Go now, leave your sire in peace."

"Da, you rode out to hunt yesterday morn, were gone until midday, and brought back not so much as a hare. You did not take any of the men with you to hunt, none knew where you had gone, or how to find you. Never have I seen you go to hunt without bringing back enough to feed us for days, and never alone! What is it, Da?"

"Very well. Since you will not leave it, since you insist you must know of my pain, I will tell you of my pain. When your mam left this world, I thought I would not ever love another woman. My heart turned to stone and I could not think of another taking your mother's place. I do not speak of a woman to ease my nights, I speak of one who would share my life, one who would *be* my life."

"I know, Da. We all felt your pain, saw how mam's death changed you. But when you met Deirdre all that changed. When first we found her, I thought I might have her for myself. I will admit I was angry that you took her for yourself. You being, you know, old, and she being of an age for me... Now Da, don't scowl at me so, it was but a brief thought. When I saw the change she wrought in you, when I saw how you each looked at the other, I knew the Goddess had brought you together. It was meant to be!"

"Aye, it is just as I believed as well. I had no more set my eyes upon her than I felt my heart begin to live again. I do not want you to think I shall ever forget your mam, but this woman has taken such a hold upon me that I never thought possible. I feel such for her as I have never felt for another, not even your mam. And I believe I will not survive should she leave me. Just the thought of her leaving me brings me such pain I cannot breathe. When I think of her out there somewhere, living without me, perhaps loving some other, being touched and sharing a bed with another, I feel such a rage, I could kill."

"And why should she leave you, Da? I can see the feelings she has for you. Sure, it is there for all to see upon her face whenever she looks at you. Whenever you are together, she touches you constantly, caresses you arm, and touches your hand."

"And yet, I believe she will leave me. She has kept herself from me these many days now. I know, I know, it may just be her woman's time, but still I feel it in my bones she waits only for the right time to tell me she will go."

"No, Da. No. She will not leave you. I know this."

"You are a good man, Naoisi. You make me proud you are my son." Grasping his son's shoulder, Niall sought to ease his son's distress. "I am sure you are right. It is just my need for assurance of her love for me that causes this confusion. Go now. I will take one of the small *curragh* across to the island. I will not be long."

"Are you sure? I can go with you, Da. I do not like to leave you alone like this."

"Go on with you. Didn't I see a bright-eyed *cailín* following you about these last few days."

"Aye, Nuala. She's a beauty, isn't she then?"

"She's Ciran's youngest, isn't she? A good match that." He would have to remember to speak of this match with Ciran when he returned.

Shoving off from the shore, Niall waved his son back to the village. He needed the time alone to think. In spite of what he had said to Naoisi, he still had the feeling of foreboding that Deirdre would tell him soon of her intent to return to her own country.

As he walked the grassy verge of the island, Niall thought of ways to make Deirdre stay with him. He could lock her away, he would never allow her out of his sight, she would be guarded day and night, but that would make him no better than Conochar. Forcing her to love him, when she did not.

He saw the little boat with Ciran and Deirdre in it leave the shore and head toward the island, and he knew in his heart the time had come. Never a man to lack courage, he came forward to face the inevitable. If she would come here to tell him she had decided to return to her own people, he would not turn and run from it, but face her decision head on, like a man, as would be expected of the Chieftain of the Eman Macha.

Helping her from the small craft, he was loath to release her hand and kept it in his as they made their way through the long pasture grasses.

She made conversation with him, spoke of banal things, and tried to compose herself. The suspense was too much for him and he could see this was difficult for her as well. Then he would make it easier for her and bring it out into the open himself.

"What is it you've come to tell me, Deirdre?" She looked him in the eye, and it tore at his heart to see the anguish there on her face. That is when it came to him like a revelation. *She does not want to leave me.* He thought, *but for some unknown reason, feels she must.* Somehow, instinctively, Niall knew that this too, was the blame of Cathub, and silently cursed the old man yet again. He would have to help her see that this is where she belonged, here with *their* people, here in his arms, bringing *his* children into the world.

"*A ghrá mo chroí,* love of my heart. You are mine. You cannot leave me. I will not survive if you leave me." Niall took Deirdre's hand in his own, put it to his lips and inhaled deeply of that scent which would forever linger in his mind.

She trembled, and he felt her uncertainty. Tenderly, Niall removed her gown, gazed upon her nakedness, and marveled at what was his. What he stood to lose. He took his woman; laid her upon the grass of this land that would be the home he would build for her and their children.

The sun shone warm upon their naked bodies. The long grasses scented the air. The water birds called out to their mates, and the Goddess looked down upon them and smiled. Time seemed to stand still, this moment, and this small piece of their world was perfect, right here, right now. If only he could make it stand still and remain thus forever.

He made love to Deirdre there upon their island, used his body to please her again and again; abandoned himself to her needs. By now, he knew her body so well, he knew just the right touch to bring her to the very edge of release and to hold her there, prolonging the pleasure, drawing out her ecstasy.

He also prayed to whatever gods or goddesses there were, that he would be enough for her, that he could make her see that her love for him was all they needed, as his love for her would sustain and keep her. He prayed also for a child, that the seed he sent forth would take root and grow within her.

And he took his pleasure of her as well. He consumed her, fed upon her, and in turn gave all of himself back to her. There was no more he could do.

She screamed her pleasure into his ear as he murmured his love into hers. "My heart, my heart, my heart".

# *Twenty-nine*

*Farewell*

*I must at least tell him good-bye and explain why I am leaving him.* Deirdre thought to herself. *I couldn't live with myself if I were to just leave without telling him, and the others, why.* Deirdre went looking for Niall in the Great Hall. Once Niall had been told, she would go to Moira and say goodbye to her as well. Saying goodbye to the others would be too difficult, and she was too much a coward to even try.

Not finding him there, she asked Naoisi where his father could be found.

"Da went out to the island. He said something about finding the best sites for building." He seemed anxious, concerned.

"What is it, Naoisi? Is something wrong?"

"Ah sure, what could be wrong. Isn't it a beautiful day, yes? A perfect day for lovers, yes?"

"Sure, I guess so. You say your father is out on the island? Will you take me out to him? I must speak with him immediately."

"Aye, of course, but its Ciran there that handles the *curragh* like he was born in one." As Naoisi pointed out the short, squat figure of Niall's best friend, Deirdre thanked him and went to Ciran.

"Ciran, I must speak with Niall. Naoisi tells me he is on the island, will you take me there?"

"Aye. He'll be pleased that you seek him out. He has done naught but sulk these many day past." Deirdre was sure her face reflected the guilty feelings that overcame her.

Their trip out to the island passed quickly as Ciran's amiable conversation filled the time, leaving none for awkward silences.

Niall must have seen their approach, as he met them at the little jetty that had been fashioned from stones found on the island.

"Thank you, Ciran. Niall will bring me back, you don't need to wait for me."

Taking Niall's hand, Deirdre walked with him up the gentle slopes of the grassy verdure. Suddenly reluctant to broach the subject that had brought her to the island, Deirdre sought idle conversation.

"Naoisi tells me you intend to build out here. This would be a wonderful place to build a stronghold. No one would be able to approach the island without being spotted and the boggy bottom of the lake makes a perfect protective border."

"My very thought. There is enough land here to build a Great Hall twice the size of the current one, and more than enough land for homes and cattle."

"You're right. I can't think of a more perfect spot." She felt the awkward, stilted tension between them. They had never been so uncomfortable with each other, even when they had first met.

"What is it you've come to tell me, Deirdre? You make idle talk, but your face hides nothing, *Cailín* and I have known for these three days past that you struggle with something. You have decided to leave me, yes?"

"I don't want to Niall, but I cannot stay here. I do not belong here."

"Why do you say you do not belong here? Have my people not made you one of their own? Do my children not call you Mother already? What is it that displeases you?"

Taking her hand, pressing it to his lips, his voice husky from the emotion that tore at his heart, "Do *I* not please you?"

Her own voice shook as Deirdre answered, "Please me? You please me too much. You make it so difficult for me to do what I know I must. I cannot leave you and yet I must."

His breath was hot against her palm where Niall still held it against his lips. "Then let me make it impossible."

Releasing her hand, Niall gently removed her gown. She thought to protest, but the words died in her throat as he lay her upon the ground.

Niall removed his own clothing, then knelt over her. Taking her hand again in his, Niall's lips and tongue touched gently against her palm, tracing wet circles then trailing down to her wrist where his lips lingered, feeling her pulse as it quickened. Guiding her arms up to encircle his neck, Niall brought his mouth down to hers, tenderly caressing her lips with his own, then his tongue tantalized and teased. Always their lovemaking had been wild and frenzied, but now Niall seemed to make an extra effort to take his time to prolong the pleasure, bringing her again and again to the very brink of release only to back away from the edge. Finally, agonizingly, the urgency of Niall's lovemaking escalated, and her heart beat quickened and breath shortened in response.

Deirdre felt as thought she were a banquet and Niall a man long without food. He fed upon her mouth, drank from her lips, took his own pleasure from her body as he consumed her. As Niall parted and entered her, his thrusting energy laying claim to her over and over again, he whispered into her ear.

"*A ghrá mo chroí.* You are mine. You are mine. You cannot leave me. I will not survive if you leave me."

Deirdre clung to Niall, as would a drowning woman cling to the shore. She let the wave that was Niall crash over her again and again, as would the waves of a tumultuous sea. Her own climax rose to meet his, drowning them both.

Deirdre lay back on the soft grass, her breath coming in ragged gasps, the salty taste of Niall's sweaty skin tingling on her tongue. She held his head as he buried his face against the soft fullness of her belly, tasting of Deirdre's own salty skin. Her nipples ached to be taken between his lips and suckled. Her entire body ached for him. Her knees drew up of their own volition, opening herself for him once again. His mouth lingered, moving slowly, taking his time, touching her first there, then here, his breath whispered against the crisp curly silk between her legs, then moved to taste the soft pliant skin of her inner thigh. Her mind screamed at him, *take me, take me, do not ever allow me to leave you.*

The satiny soft stroke of Niall's tongue brought an involuntary quiver that ran the length of her; electric waves of pleasure. Deirdre tensed and arched as Niall moved boldly, placing his mouth upon her, sending her over the edge. Her body exploded into uncontrollable spasms.

As she fell back once again to the grass, panting heavily, Niall still did not leave her. He moved up to clamp his mouth to hers and enter her yet again. Pinning her to the earth, he possessed her again, and yet again, murmuring, "*mo chroí, mo chroí, mo chroí*" again and again, while their bodies moved in the eternal rhythm nature dictated.

Stretching and arching her back luxuriously like a cat, Deirdre purred in contentment. Reveling in the sensuous feel of her lover's touch, she refused to think beyond this the physical gratification he gave to her at this moment.

It was hours later—Deirdre did not know how much time had lapsed since she and Niall had finally collapsed in each others arms—she sat some small distance from him, watching as he slept, arms tossed casually about his head, legs sprawled, as only a man who is deeply satisfied and content can.

Deirdre hugged her knees to her with her arms, her head dropped to her knees, and she wept.

# *Thirty*

## *The Gathering of the Clans*

Two seasons had passed since Conochar and the Ulaid were driven from the lands of Niall's people, now known as *Uí Neill.* And who were forever split from the Ulaid. The cattle raids that marked the past two years had stopped. The Bards composed epic poems that told of the love, and death, of Deirdre and Niall, and the disgrace of Conochar.

In the spring the clans gather as they have always done, long into the past, and will continue to do long into the mists of the future. It is a time of welcoming new life into the clan, honoring the aged, speaking of betrothals and acknowledging the joining of two people in marriage. The gathering continues for many days, as there are many new babes that come to the clan, it has been a good winter and many will plight their troth or join their hands. Each celebration, each special event must be given their due before the heads of all the tribes.

Niall stands tall upon the great stone wall that surrounds the newly completed Great Hall, constructed upon the island sanctuary of the *Uí Neill*, now called *Inishmacha.* The island has been named thus in honor of the patron goddess *Macha*, who the people believe sent Deirdre to them to give her life to save the *Uí Neill* from the Ulaid.

It had proven to be such a safe refuge during the invasion of the Ulaid, Niall decided to move the *Uí Neill* stronghold to the island. The walls that surround and protect this newly constructed stronghold are twice the breadth of the old compound walls and taller by the height of one man.

The Great Hall itself, rather than having just a sleeping loft, boasts a full second floor with stone steps leading to it. Niall has taken up residence there on the second floor, for guests are now housed in the old Great Hall on the mainland, now the *Uí Neill* Guest Hall.

Separate dwellings have been built for Naoisi, now newly married; his own joining to be celebrated at the gathering, as well as Ardan, his wife and new child, and other storage buildings and stables.

The *Uí Neill* cattle now graze upon the lush grasses of the island.

A causeway of massive timber, brought up from the great forests of the west and driven deep into the boggy lake bottom, reaches out into the lake, marking the only safe access to the island.

Niall watched tents spring up on the grassy verge surrounding the old village compound as the clans begin to arrive, and prepared himself to return to the mainland for the gathering.

He thought with pride, and no small amount of sadness, upon Levarcham, his only daughter, as she also prepares. She is to be betrothed this day to Maírtín, eldest son of the Chieftain of the *Hy Drona*, a tribe well to the southeast. It does not sit well with Niall to have his child promised so far from him, but she does have her heart set on the match. His only consolation is that he would have Levie with him one more year before she is to be wed.

Ilam, now ten and two, would also be taking leave of Niall, although it was for just the short distance across the lake. For the coming years he would live with the two aging Druids of the *Uí Neill*, learning the art of the Druid. The boy had shown a talent for storytelling and set his mind to becoming a Bard of the Druidic order.

Descending from the fortified wall, Niall spots his friend coming towards him.

"Ah Ciran, it has been a year of change, has it not?"

"Hasn't it just. And change is good, yes?"

"Aye, but that does not mean it must always be welcome."

Clapping his friend and Chieftain on the back, Ciran chided Niall, "This is a joyful day! Let us gather your family together and join the clans. The *curragh* awaits and I grow restive."

Laughing, Niall throws his arm about his friend's shoulder and they enter the Great Hall together.

"I take that to mean it has been over long since your last meal, old friend."

"Aye, my lord, and as my chieftain is it not your duty to correct this?"

"You forget, I am chieftain no longer. Naoisi is this day to become Chieftain of the *Uí Neill.*"

"Aye, but you shall always have my first loyalty, Niall mac Usna."

Laughing, they entered the new Great Hall.

"There is my Levie." Niall beamed as Levarcham, resplendent in her newly made gown of finely spun wool, dyed just the right shade of amber, made her way down the mural stair that led from the sleeping rooms above. The women had been up since dawn making her ready for her betrothed. He then moved quickly to help when he spotted the lumbering figure that grasped Levie's outstretched hand, supported from behind by Niambh and Moira.

Once the waddling figure had safely negotiate the steep stairs, Niall surrounded his wife with his arms and tenderly placed his hands upon Deirdre's swollen belly, where his child grew.

Turning to Ciran, Niall said, "Yes, my friend, change is indeed good."

Following Deirdre's eye, Niall noticed she looked long upon the Druid's Crystal, which she had insisted be hung from the highest beams of the Great Hall.

"Do you change your mind, *Cailín*? Do you wish me to retrieve Cathub's crystal?"

Leaning into the strong supportive arms of her husband, Deirdre signed contentedly, "No. I just like to look upon it and know that the world Cathub would have forced upon me can no longer touch me. It reminds me of what has been given to me and what I very nearly threw away."

"Let us proceed to the gathering. The clans assemble and there is news to be heard, and to be told."

Helping his wife into the little *curragh* that would carry them to the shore, Niall thought back to the day Deirdre had come to this island to make her farewell to him.

Supporting Deirdre's back against his chest and rubbing his hands across the swollen belly where his new son grew, feeling the life kicking and thrusting against Deirdre's stomach. Niall asked for what was not the first time. He never tired of hearing her answer.

"*Mo Chroí,* what is it made you decide to stay with me that day? I know you had come to tell me you would not stay with me, what is it changed you mind?"

"I looked at you as you slept. I saw your contentment. I knew that I had given that peace to you. And I asked myself how I could leave you. I had argued with myself for three days prior, saying always the same thing. How can I leave this man? He gives me everything he has and asks only that I stand beside him and love him, how can I leave him? And I realized, if I had to ask this question of myself over and over again, and still did not find an answer, perhaps the reason was because I asked the wrong question. Better I should ask myself, why *should* I leave this man? The answer came to me immediately; there is no good reason to leave him... you. So, I decided to stay, and let you give me babies."

"Aye, babies. This child of mine who grows within you will be a strong son. See how he seeks to release himself into the world."

"Son? How do you know it is a son I carry? Perhaps I shall give you a daughter."

"Yes, a daughter. I would like another daughter. A girl I can spoil in my old age. She shall have her father's courage and her mother's beauty and intelligence. A red-haired warrior woman who will tame any man who dare to think he might have her. What shall we name this daughter?"

"Aisling, I want to name her Aisling."

# *Epilogue*

## *The Legend*

There was much drinking and celebration in the house of Fedlimid, son of Dall. The wife of Fedlimid, though she was great with child, served the men of the Ulaid, and their King, Conochar, for it was a great honor to the house of her husband that the King should choose their home for his celebration.

The wife of Fedlimid felt the child move within her womb, and was stricken with both fear and excitement that her time drew near.

Seeing that Cathub, most exalted of all Druids, attended upon the King, the wife of Fedlimid approached and begged that he place his hand upon her swollen belly that he might tell her of the fate of the child.

When Cathub placed his hand so, the child did call out to him of what was to be. "It is a female child you carry and she cries out to me in sorrow," he said. "A child who will grow to great beauty and charm. A braid of long red hair and eyes of green, small of stature and clean of limb shall she be; however, great sorrow will come to the men of the Ulaid on her account. A great slaughter will take place in her name, and the greatest of Kings will do battle for her hand. You shall call her Derdriu and her great beauty shall bring suffering and shame to the Ulaid."

The warriors of Conochar rose up with a great hue and cry, and demanded the child be put to death, but the King refused.

After the child was born, Conochar would have it that Derdriu should be kept for him until she was of an age to be wed. The midwife let it be known to the wife of Fedlimid that the child had died of the milk fever, and Derdriu was placed into the hands of Cathub, to be raised in isolation, away from all, and educated in all ways as is fitting the wife of a great King.

As the babe grew to womanhood, she did fulfill the Druid's prophesy in her great beauty.

When Derdriu did reach a marriageable age, Conochar sent forth three of his princes, sons of Usna, to bring his bride to him. The eldest of Usna's sons did set his heart upon Derdriu when first he had sight of her. That night he took her hand as his own, and carried Derdriu back to the land of his fathers...

...So great was the rage and jealousy of Conochar that the King did send the many warriors of the Ulaid to pursue the two lovers and laid siege across all of Eire. A great battle ensued, fully three hundred Ulaid fell and the lands of Usna's sons was set to fire, but still Derdriu was not taken.

Conochar would have it that the great Druid Cathub use his magic to destroy the sons of Usna, but it was to no avail. Still the wall of the *Uí Neill* stood against the King.

When it was discovered by Conochar he could not have Derdriu by force, he determined to take her by cunning.

Fedlimid was sent to parlay a peace with the son's of Usna, and when they did come forth to speak of peace with Conochar, they were struck down by point of sword. Seeing her husband lying thus in his grave, Derdriu did lie herself down beside her beloved and, as she did so, the breath left her breast and they did see that Derdriu was dead.

The Lady of the Moon let it be known that She would no longer shine upon the traitorous Conochar, and so it was that the Lady of the Moon did turn Her back upon the men of the Ulaid. The warriors of the Ulaid rose up against Conochar for they did see that their King was not a man of honor, which they prized above all else, and they would follow his rule no longer.

Conochar was driven from the lands of the *Uí Neill* never to return.

# *Gaelic names*

*and how to pronounce them*

Ardan (*Aart*-an)
Arguile (*Ar*-gile)
Cathub (Ca-*tuv*)
Ciran (*Kiiar*-on)
Conochar (*Cona*-kar)
Derdriu or Deirdre (*Deer*-dre)
Fedlimid (*Feyd*-lim)
Fionna (Fee-*o*-nah)
Ilam (*E*-lam)
Levarcham (Lev-*ar*-ham)
Maire (Mary)
Naoisi (*Nay*-see)
Niall (Neal)
Niambh (Neev)
Nuala (Noola)
Pádraig (Patrick)